A MOTHER'S TORMENT

BY

XAVIER POE KANE

C2 VISIONARY PRESS, LLC
ST. LOUIS, MISSOURI

Also by Xavier Poe Kane

The Hidden Lives of Dick & Mary: Two Novellas of
Supernatural Suspense

Broken Hearts & Other Horrors

For K. V.;

Every story has many sides, and the truth is often somewhere in the middle.

Our minds, our sanity
we try to keep,

but the world is a pit
two black holes deep,

and off the edge
we try to leap.

So if I should wake before I die,
tell me to go back to sleep.

— Kayla Randolph,
"Asleep But Alive"

Prologue

February 25, 2018

Knock. Knock. Knock.

June Reuter thrashed as the noise from inside the wall tried to wake her.

Knock. Knock. Knock.

Her mind clawed to stay in a deep and dreamless sleep, but the discordant sound jarred her awake. Giving up the battle, she opened her eyes—a striking green.

They were the only good things inherited from her biological father. (Her mother and stepfather just called him "the sperm donor.") She hated looking in the mirror otherwise, seeing his features. She wished she had her mother's instead of those of a man who abused and abandoned her and her mother when she was too young to even remember his face. She'd even wished she looked like her stepfather, Michael. At least then

11

her features would remind her of someone who loved her and not a stranger.

Knock. Knock. Knock.

The terrible hammering reminded her of yesterday's pain. Alexis was supposed to be her friend. She had known that Ethan was the boy June was crushing on, but apparently, that hadn't mattered to Alexis—June caught her making out with him behind a barn during a homeschool co-op outing. Another girl captured the moment and spread it on social media where other kids added their two cents to the feed, so even being home provided no distance or respite from the betrayal. She spent the evening locked in her room, eyes full of tears and glued to her phone.

Knock. Knock. Knock.

"I'm awake! Is that what you want?" she cried.

Knock. Knock. Knock.

"Is this it?" she whimpered.

June longed to be loved by someone other than her family. Someone who chose her for who she was and not out of obligation or reciprocated filial piety. She checked her feed once more, hoping to find a friend who was online and might offer some kindness. She instead found a picture of Ethan and Alexis. Alexis had added text: "Me and you, baby." June burst into tears.

Knock. Knock. Knock.

As if a flip switched in her mind, she became comfortably numb. The pain left. A cold logic began to form, swiftly replacing her adolescent despondency. Her thoughts became clear and calm.

"There is no pain in the nothingness," she whispered, suddenly aware of the cold, dark embrace of the ether and the comfort and peace it could offer her. She possessed awareness but not control as she slipped out of bed.

I know what you're thinking. It's not worth it. A masculine voice splintered through her mind. *I know. It's not worth it. I thought it would fix my problems, too. It didn't.*

June tried to argue but could not find her voice. She succumbed to silence. She was only faintly aware of the familiar sound of stairs creaking as she floated down into the kitchen. She knew the tile floor should be cold on her bare feet, but she did not feel it.

It's not worth it. Think of the people who love you. Trust me.

June tried to scream, but her mouth did not form words. She only managed to violently shake her head. The voice refused to stop cajoling her.

Put it down.

She did not know what she needed to put down. The creak of her feet on the stairs rejoined the voice. Something glinted in her hands.

It's not you. Others hurt you, betrayed you. Don't let their wickedness defeat you.

She heard the grating, loud protest of antique hinges opening and closing. The click of the lock secured her inside her bathroom. An ornate pedestal sink stood silent guard over the clawfoot tub and the pull-chain toilet original to the room, but to June it felt practically clinical, sterile. It reeked of Lysol and bleach. She was surrounded by pure white towels. She faintly acknowledged the sound of pipes clattering as she turned on the water.

Knock. Knock. Knock.

Even here, the knocking in the walls would not give her peace. The calm numbness shattered for a moment, but it helped. It silenced the voice that blocked the way to peace.

The blade bit into her skin. Detached, she watched red water swirl before disappearing into the black hole of the sink's drain. She watched passively as the knife sunk into her wrist once more. Deeper this time but not quite deep enough. Each slice brought her closer. She became light-headed. She began to float away.

There's still time. You have The Circle.

"Shut the fuck up!" she screamed, vocal cords finally stirred to life.

She examined herself in the mirror. Tears flowed from bloodshot eyes. The blade cut into her flesh once more. Part of her wanted to stop, but that part was not in control.

She heard a distant banging, different from the knocking. She thought she heard a different voice, but she could not understand it. The latch bolt splintered, and the door flew open.

Michael stood frozen with a shocked expression. "June! What the fuck!"

That's strange. Daddy never cusses.

"Lillian!"

His voice was loud.

14

"Bring the Goddamned first aid kit! Our daughter needs you!"

Daddy never takes the Lord's name in vain.

§

Lillian rushed out of her bedroom and down the hall toward the light streaming out of their daughter's bathroom. She saw June's bare feet and legs, her husband's robed form hovering over June's torso. She saw tears in his eyes as he held a red towel over her wrist. It was the color that caught Lillian's attention. *We don't own any red towels.* Then it clicked, and the cognitive dissonance dissipated.

"Fuck!" she yelled, kneeling over her daughter and examining the scene.

Michael's knuckles turned white as he applied direct pressure on the wound that was bleeding the most. Lillian noticed several cuts. The hesitation cuts—made as the teen willed herself to slice deeper—only trickled blood and, for the moment, could be ignored.

"Hold her arm above her heart." She forced a calm tone into her voice, and Michael immediately obeyed.

Lillian's heart pounded in her chest. Tears slid down her cheeks as she set to work saving her daughter's life. Her own breathing was heavy as she watched June's becoming weaker. Her mind calculated how much blood June had lost. Most of the shallow cuts ran parallel to veins and arteries, but the two deepest ran lengthwise and were closer to her blood vessels. Had

15

Michael slept 10 seconds later, there would have been no hope.

June seemed calm, but Lillian had seen that before in dying patients in the ER. She was haunted by the expression of succumbing to the momentary seduction of despair that she had seen in a young man who had slit his wrists.

"It's okay, Momma. I want to go."

Her voice was chilling, but Lillian was relieved that she was still strong enough to talk.

"But we don't want you to go!" Lillian choked back emotion.

"Jesus, please help us!" Michael begged.

June smiled.

Lillian tore into the paramedic kit, pulled out a tourniquet, and wrapped it around June's bicep. She began turning the stick-like windlass, and the black fabric tightened. She slowly cut off the blood to her daughter's lower extremities. Michael started to re-move the washcloth.

"No," she directed, "go make an ice pack!"

"Should I call 9-1-1?"

"No, we'll take her ourselves. It'll be faster. We'll take my car."

With her physician's license plates and hazards flashing, no cop would pull them over. She wrapped more gauze around the washcloth followed by a cravat to secure the dressing.

"Momma, stop crying. It's okay. I don't hurt any-more," June said blissfully. "Even the ghosts are leaving me alone."

Forcing a smile when all she wanted to do was break down and sob was the hardest thing Lillian had ever done. She caressed June's face and stared into her eyes as she brushed the blood-matted hair from her forehead. She echoed the girl's words. "It's going to be okay."

After an eternity of silence, a shadow fell over the two women. Lillian looked up to see her husband with a Ziploc bag full of ice. June stared blankly at the ceiling.

"Carry her to the car," Lillian ordered.

Michael handed Lillian the ice and lifted his step-daughter off the floor. Lillian stood and grabbed a tow-el before following Michael outside.

PART ONE:
Coming Home

I think of "ghosts" as souls that have not moved on and need a little help. Sometimes, they don't know that they're dead. Other times, they feel like they have business left undone or need to be there for someone special in their life. Sometimes they are tied through love or blinded by hate.

They can interact with the physical world in minor ways. I've been pushed, scratched, and felt them inside me making me feel some internal injuries. Perhaps a taste of what took their life. But their ability to do harm is often very limited.

— Dick Fisher, Spirit Medium
Co-host, *Haunted Houses*

I

August 2026

A month had passed since Lillian received a call from her sobbing daughter saying her marriage was over. It required a little motherly persuasion, but her baby decided to come home. Despite being a cheating lowlife, Robert did the right thing and agreed not to contest the divorce or June's move back to Missouri from Atlanta. In the separation agreement, he got the house and she took his prized Dodge Charger SRT Hellcat—an act of spite that made Lillian smirk with pride.

She was currently working from home on a presentation for the annual meeting of the National Organization of State Offices of Rural Health when a sharp pain interrupted her thoughts.

"I need to buy a better chair," she muttered as the familiar pain shot through her abdomen. She squirmed as the pain rescinded, her blouse making a soft rustling sound.

The presentation concerned her hospital's reaction to the 2020 novel coronavirus pandemic. She had studied the reports coming out of China in late 2019. In January 2020, she had watched streaming videos of government-built hospitals popping up like Starbucks. A lesser physician would have shrugged and thought it merely interesting, but something had itched at the back of Lillian's mind.

One of her old professors often reminded his students: "When you hear hoofbeats, think horses not zebras." It was a familiar admonishment to not give in to flights of fancy and to be mindful of Occam's razor: Between two possible diagnoses, the simpler one is usually correct. Lillian often ignored this sage advice and made conclusions her peers would avoid or never think of. Her clever mind refused relegation to any box. When the pandemic struck the U.S., her independent streak would be credited with saving many lives.

As she glanced away from her computer, her gaze fell upon a photograph of her and her adopted parents. Sometimes she wondered what life could have been if she had grown up in Korea. Lillian always admired her birth name, Yi Joon-hee, so she named her daughter June Lee.

A gunshot in the distance caused Lillian to gaze out her window. At first, she thought Michael had decided to get some last-minute shooting in before their daughter and grandson arrived. An unsecured handgun in the house was fine when it was just them, but they were about to have a four-year-old child in the home and their once-suicidal daughter. Lillian insisted he put his revolver in a proper safe if either was home.

Instead, she saw a military funeral taking place on the 40 acres adjacent to her property, the honor guard on point. The first volley fired by seven riflemen managed to sound like a single gunshot. A second volley followed, but one member being slightly off made it sound like two shots in rapid succession. The team was once more on point with the third and final volley.

They lived in a renovated National Guard armory that she and her husband inherited from her grandfather. The government converted part of the land into a cemetery before he purchased it. Her heart sank at the memory of burying her parents there after a car accident took them from her. The sound of tires crunching on gravel roused her from the sad memories. Lillian smiled as her former son-in-law's Dodge pulled up the driveway.

"Michael! June is home!"

She heard her husband hurry to the top of the stairs on the second floor.

"I'm on my way!" he yelled in excitement.

Lillian's second husband Michael legally adopted June once her first husband surrendered his parental rights. The sperm donor long ago drifted out of their lives. She was sure the man didn't know he had a grandson.

Michael joined her as she watched June release a fussy child from his car seat.

"Oh my God, she cut and dyed her hair," Lillian whispered, gripping her husband's arm.

June's long raven hair was reduced to a short bob dyed a wine-colored red.

"Don't say anything. She had to make a change. Compliment her."

Lillian understood the need to reinvent oneself after the end of a relationship.

§

June took a moment to collect her thoughts and courage. Her mother appeared at the door.

"It's time," she whispered to herself.

With a deep breath, she opened the door and started waking Mikey. She struggled with his crankiness at being woken early, but her mother closed the distance with outstretched arms.

"Welcome home, princess." Her mom embraced her and Mikey.

"Thanks, Mom," June said—a conscious choice. Ever since the night she had tried to kill herself, she called Lillian "Mom" instead of "Momma." It put more distance between them and that memory.

Lillian was her rock, though she was terrified at how Lillian would react to her hair. Her mother was fiercely proud of their Korean heritage and that included their long, black hair. June worried she had rocked the boat too much too soon.

"It's time," she whispered to herself.

Without a rich husband paying tuition, she could no longer afford her expensive private school in another state. Plus, it made sense for the newly single mom to be close to family while completing her undergraduate degree—economics—that would now take place at the University of Missouri-Kansas City.

While June and her mother embraced, the sandstone two-story house cast the shadow of a Gothic castle over the reunion. June peered up at her childhood home. Two brick chimneys jutted in defiance on either side of the house. On both sides of the doorway, a turret reached into the sky. The two heavy doors were made of local hardwood. After a long moment, Lillian let her go. Her mother touched her hair, and June held her breath as she waited for the fury.

"I like it."

"Really?"

"Yes! Why wouldn't I?"

June considered her mother, bewildered.

"Can a dad get some attention, too?" Her father clutched her in a tight bear hug. "I'm so glad to have you back, kiddo."

"Paw-Paw!" Mikey cried out to his namesake, latching onto his favorite grandparent's leg.

He released her and picked up her son. "Hey, Mikey! I bet you'd love to go play, wouldn't you?"

"Let's go play!" the toddler squealed.

"I'll let you ladies get settled while I try to spoil and wear out this little boy."

June watched as her father carried the boy off to June's newly refurbished childhood swing set.

Her mother wrapped her arm around her and led her into the house. "Come, let's head to the kitchen. I'll make you some herbal tea."

It was a mother-daughter tradition that began when June was in middle school and first began battling Myalgic encephalomyelitis, or ME. Older professionals knew it as chronic fatigue syndrome. The disease presented after a severe flu when she was 12. June's trouble sleeping began soon after, as well as trouble in school. Once a straight-A student like her mother, her grades had begun to slip.

They decided to withdraw her from public school, favoring a private school in the suburbs of Kansas City near the insurance company where Michael worked as an actuary. But after the first year, he tallied the numbers. Between June's after-school care and the time missed at work to attend school functions, he realized working did not make much sense. He'd saved well over the years, and the family decided it would be for the best if he quit and got engaged with the local homeschool co-op. This worked out well for June who, despite the disease, once more began excelling academically.

"How have you been feeling?" Lillian queried as they walked back to the house.

"Oh. I think the symptoms are coming back because of all the emotions with the divorce and the back and forth as I decided what to do. I'm doing all right though, not nearly as bad as it used to be."

XAVIER POE KANE

Lillian hugged her daughter. "It will be fine. Let Mom make you some tea, and we will get everything back in order."

June grinned, happy to have a mother who always helped make everything better. She studied the house. Out of the corner of her eye, she glimpsed a figure in the dining room window. She jerked her head toward the window, but all she could see was the fluttering of the curtain as the sun glinted off the glass. A shiver ran down her spine. Something else had decided to welcome her home.

II

"Mom, Grandpa Charlie is here!" June's voice echoed throughout the house as she rushed to open the door. She flung the door open and looked up to Charlie Peterson, her pseudo-grandfather. She jumped up and wrapped her arms around his neck.

He wrapped one arm around her in a hug, holding a paper bag in his other hand. "Okay, June-Bug," he laughed, failing to cover up the sound of his back cracking as he straightened. "You're not a little girl anymore, and I'm not as young as I used to be."

"I'm sorry. I'm just happy to see you!"

"I know, it's great to have you back! I'm really sorry to hear about Robert. What a fuckin' dick."

June sighed, the urge to defend Robert coexisted with the urge to agree with Charlie. "Yeah, but I'm home and want to put that in the past. I just want to move forward."

"I gotcha, June-Bug."

She felt a rush of comfortable nostalgia as he gave her a peck on the top of the head like he'd done when she was a child. Charlie's daughter Sarah was her mother's childhood best friend. Sarah, in turn, was the mother of June's best friend Gerica. When June's grandparents died, Charlie helped fill the void. Over the decades, the families had grown so close that they attended each other's family reunions.

"What'd you bring me?" she asked as he held up the bag.

"I stopped at Higgin's Gas for gas and some wine."

She took the bag and pulled out one of two bottles of wine.

"I've missed St. James Winery! Robert's family were snobs and turned up their noses at Missouri wine." She turned the bottle around in her hand as if it were a Bordeaux from Thomas Jefferson's wine cellar.

"This won't go with Michael's lasagna, but it'll make a great dessert wine." She turned and led him to the dining room.

"Charlie," said Lillian, embracing him as June had. "Great to see you again!"

"Look, Mom! He brought wine," June said, holding up the bottles.

"Michael won't drink any," Lillian observed.

"More for us," June giggled.

June felt the safe warmth of home as Charlie slipped a hand around her and Lillian's waist as they walked to the dining room.

"So how are my favorite Reuter girls doing? Staying out of trouble? June, are you beating the boys off with a stick at school?"

"The semester only started Wednesday. Besides, I like older men."

"She'd better watch herself. Don't need another Robert situation," her mother chimed in.

Charlie shook his head in disbelief. "It's good to see some things will never change."

June felt his beer belly jiggle as he chuckled.

§

As the main course wound down, June watched as Charlie leaned back in his seat to let his two helpings of lasagna settle. Michael silently began clearing the dishes.

"Gerica is going to be so excited to see you, June-Bug."

"I haven't told her I'm back home yet."

"Oh? Why not? She'd love to see you and the rug rat."

She looked down at her plate to avoid Charlie's cocked eyebrow. "I'm not ready to face my friends."

"Gerica's not just your friend, she's family. You've always been like sisters. And she's worried about you. You can't move back to a place like Junction Falls and expect people not to notice. It's not Atlanta."

"Well, the phone calls both ways," she barked.

"Hey, I'm just the messenger. When I told her I was having dinner over here, she asked if I'd mention it. She asked me to do it *delicately*." He caught her eyes with his, a bit of mirth twinkling in them. "Now, I don't know if I am being delicate or like a bull in a china shop." He placed one of his big rancher's paws on her hand.

As it engulfed hers, a warm wave of love washed over her.

"I'm just saying, get in touch. Reconnect. People'll start to talk and get the wrong impression. They'll say Atlanta changed you and now you're putting on airs."

June looked at her mother for rescue, who softly cleared her throat.

"June is figuring a few things out and easing back into the rhythm and flow of Junction Falls."

She relaxed as his gaze shifted to Lillian.

"I know, and I get that. But they can help her heal from this. They want to help her heal. It's what we do around here. I know you're a doctor, but I didn't think med school took that much of your common sense."

June stifled a laugh. She couldn't help but take a small measure of satisfaction in how Charlie could cow Lillian. It was nice to see her mother in the presence of someone who could stand up to her. June turned her gaze toward her son.

"Yeah, like figuring out what it is about men—" she caught herself, clearing her throat before continuing. "How certain men want to leave their children."

"Robert hasn't been calling to talk to Mikey that much," Lillian interjected.

June caught a knowing look shared by her mother and Charlie and made a mental note to press him on what he knows about her own absent father.

"How much is he calling?" he asked.

"Oh, every other day or less," June answered, "but every night Mikey wants to say good night or have his daddy read him a book before bed."

"Daddy?" Mikey, bored by the conversation, looked up at her when he heard the word.

"Maybe we should stick a pin in this," Lillian suggested.

Michael stepped in from the shadows of the kitchen.

"I can take him, got a new *Lil' Christians* book about John the Baptist to read to him before bed."

June noted a familiar flash of irritation bordering on rage pass across her mother's face, then it was gone.

She helped Mikey down from his seat before turning her attention back to Charlie, who was eyeing Michael carrying the boy to bed. She realized as she got older that Charlie never fully accepted Michael's ability to exist in her mother's shadow. And while she remembered a time when Grandpa Charlie's visits became less common because of that sexist attitude, it thankfully proved only a temporary bump in the road. The relationship mended, and they moved forward as an extended family.

"Look at Michael." June picked up her line of thought and addressed Charlie. "Look at you. Not only were you a father to Sarah but a second father to Mom. So how could Robert abandon Mikey? Or how could the sperm—" she cut herself off, almost deciding not to finish her statement when she saw Lillian's annoyed look. "Or how could the donor abandon me?" Her gaze lowered to the table as the sad weight of her questions settled on the room.

Charlie shifted uncomfortably in his chair. "Well, I like to believe that more men are like Michael and me than Robert and the sperm donor."

It was her mother's turn to squirm.

June suddenly felt like she was drowning in her emotions, in her desperate need for answers. She had never expected to raise a child alone, and she wondered if her mother had felt the same way. She just wanted to understand. "You knew him, didn't you?" Her voice cracked as she grasped at the hope of Charlie's insight.

Charlie sighed deeply. "June-Bug, I—"

"Can we talk about something else? Please?" Lillian begged, her voice uncharacteristically feeble.

"But Mom, I want to know!" June slammed a fist on the table, causing glassware, plates, and silverware to rattle. "I need to know about my biological father. I need to know as a mom in the same situation as you!" She locked eyes with her mother, a rare challenge for her.

"June, you are *not* in the same situation as me!" Lillian made no effort to hide the anger and disgust in her voice.

"Mom—"

"June," Michael said, entering the dining room, "Mikey is asking for you."

"We'll finish this later," she said with a huff before getting up and pushing her chair in.

§

Lillian walked Charlie to the door. "I'm sorry about June—" she began before getting cut off.

"Lilly, you knew this day would come," he interrupted. "Take it from an old man, the longer you want to bury this, the worse it's going to be when she either stumbles upon something or goes behind your back to find out about him."

"Well, I'm not sure if I'm ready—"

"Lilly-Pad." His tone softened in his peculiar way, demanding her attention. "This isn't about you. This is about being a mother and even a grandmother. It's your call. I can't make you. All I can ask is you just think about it."

She sighed in frustration.

"I know you don't like to be pushed. You may've been born in Korea, but you took to stubbornness like a Missouri-born-and-raised mule. Sometimes, you do your best work only after you've been pushed."

She looked up into his eyes and tried to hold his gaze for a moment before looking away. "The past is buried. He's not a factor, and she's happier that way."

"She's happy or you're happier?"

Lillian winced, his words cutting too close to the truth. "I'll think about it."

"That's my girl."

There it was: the fatherly tone that cheered her after her first heartbreak, the death of her parents, and her divorce.

He leaned down and kissed the top of her head. "Good night, Lilly-Pad."

"Good night, Charlie."

Lillian began to shut the door when a sudden gloom gripped her heart. She had felt it only once before: the night her parents stepped out the same door and never returned home. She had been too absorbed in getting ready for her senior homecoming dance. She barely said good-bye.

She watched him walk to his truck and get in. He waved as he turned around in the driveway before turning onto the road. She stood vigil until his headlights disappeared into the darkness, a silent prayer to keep him safe.

She walked back toward the kitchen to see Michael cleaning up as June put Mikey to bed. Lillian wanted to do some more work on her COVID presentation.

"Hey, Lilly-Pad!" he called as she passed the kitchen door.

She did nothing to hide the irritation that spread across her face.

"I know, I know. That's Charlie's nickname." A playful grin splayed across his face. "But it's worth it. You're beautiful when you're angry."

"You know June would say that you're being sexist," she lilted, sauntering to the fridge.

"I've been thinking about dinner. What Charlie said to you as he—" He couldn't finish his sentence.

Lillian smugly watched him. She had resorted to a favorite trick of hers. Pulling out a container of strawberries, she took one in hand and stopped it just before it passed her lips. Michael's eyes glanced back and forth between her eyes and her mouth.

"You were eavesdropping?"

"No, honey. Charlie doesn't have a low-volume setting, and neither do you when he's around. June may have heard it upstairs."

She shrugged, annoyed, and put the strawberry on the counter.

"June isn't a child now. She's a mom and going through something *very* similar to what you went through. She could use your mentoring—not your silence."

Lillian dismissively shook her head. "June's not ready. She doesn't need this right now."

"Damn it, Lillian." He did not yell. He growled. "Stop! Just. Stop. You do a lot of talking but not enough listening."

Lillian was taken aback. "Michael—"

"No. Listen to me. She has a right to know. And what if she finds your pictures and other crap you saved?"

Lillian scoffed. "She won't. She's scared of the basement."

"That's another problem—problems, actually. First, you're a doctor and you can't get your 24-year-old daughter over her irrational fear of the dark, scary basement? Secondly, why do you even have those things down there? It's been 20 years, Lillian. You've moved on. You're happily married to me. At least, that's what you've told me."

Despite her anger, her eyes quivered as they started to well with tears. She took a deep breath. "You're right, Michael. You and Charlie have given me things to think about. It's just that I spent so much time as a single mother, so it's tough taking parenting advice from men."

"Lillian!" His face flushed crimson. "You haven't been one of those for years! And I put *my* career on hold so you could still work your dream job."

Annoyed and over the argument, she reached for the discarded strawberry. Determined, she brought it to her lips and met his gaze. "I went too far, and I'm sorry. You know, we don't have to fight if you'd rather do something else." Her voice trailed as she slowly slipped the fruit between her lips.

III

Between Mikey, her parents, and starting at a new college, there was little time for June herself to settle in. The life she left behind in Georgia had not yet been fully unpacked into the room where she grew up. She had planned on sunbathing later, but Mikey wanted to play outside now. Needing a break from the tedium and seeing clouds in the distance, she gave in and followed him outside.

As they drew close to her childhood playset, she felt the anxiety of moving fade. The late summer day was hot, so she slipped off the t-shirt over her bikini top. Without Atlanta's humidity, the heat of the sun felt good on her exposed skin. Mikey ran to the fortress side of the equipment and mounted the small rock-climbing face to slide back down.

June lay in the grass and closed her eyes, experiencing all the sensations vision can blind people to: the noise of leaves dancing in the breeze, the scent of freshly dug earth in the small cemetery downwind from her, the soft yet scratchy sensation of grass on her back and legs. Occasionally, the breeze would carry the clean taste of rain.

Like most kids who grew up in Junction Falls, her feet got itchy in high school, and she dreamed of a life beyond the nothingness of a small town. She lusted for art, culture, and sophistication. She began despising the insular, rural worldview of those whose ambitions ended at the county line. And yet here she was, back in The Circle enjoying simple pleasures. Becoming a parent changed something for her. Sidetracked career ambitions no longer seemed as important. Time spent at school or an internship meant time away from home and family. She began questioning the academic and professional rat race. Over a decade earlier, Michael walked away from his job to raise her. Not everyone required a career to achieve fulfillment.

The epiphany brought a smile to her face. This part of the yard called to her, a refuge of quiet safety. She called it The Circle, although she did not know why. It just felt correct. In a world complicated by uncertainty, this did not require further examination.

§

Lillian did not understand her daughter's fear of the basement. She dismissed June's oft-repeated complaint that it was too dark; Lillian thought the sparse lights chased the shadows away better than one would expect. Additionally, the cool floor under her bare feet provided relief from the blistering heat of a Missouri August. When her grandfather would bring her here while he worked to convert the armory into a home, she would come downstairs to play. It's even where she created her first imaginary friend, Mr. Smith. But even long after the time of imaginary friends, this was where she came when she needed to center herself. To relax. To think.

Before returning home, June had begun asking questions about the sperm donor. She considered her daughter's arguments. June was no longer a child and thought herself capable of making her own choices and protecting herself, but the question was larger than June. June would argue that she just wanted to know the name of her biological father. Lillian was too smart for that ploy. One question would lead to another until she was talking to him and hearing lies and slander. Eventually, they would want to meet, and what if June wanted to move close to him? Taking Mikey with her? Contact would be too dangerous. It would destabilize the equilibrium she had built in the years after the divorce.

As she moved through the basement, she found herself in front of the box. The unassuming banker's box collecting dust contained the remains of her worst life decision. Michael long abandoned efforts to convince her that this coffin of bad memories should go. He would protest that he understood many women her age had kept memory boxes of exes but eventually threw them out when they got married or remarried. She resisted his logic. She couldn't explain it to him, but she needed to keep it.

Lillian slid the lid off and rummaged for the picture. It had been taken on their honeymoon to Jamaica. The sperm donor towered over her, his red hair blowing in the wind. Even now, seeing his muscular, shirtless chest caused her to go weak in the knees. Lillian bit her lip, remembering the lovemaking that happened on that trip. She especially loved his shoulders. She once thought he could carry the weight of the world.

Lillian chided herself and closed her eyes, looking for the strength to resist the positive feelings that were inevitable with nostalgia. The image of a letter carefully buried in the bottom of the box entered her mind. Pulling the remaining contents aside, she found the paper in its place. She held it up and read the familiar lines.

Lillian,

The past few hours have been the most humiliating of my life. I know I haven't been the perfect husband. I'm not going to win Father of the Year. I'm wrestling with physical pain and emotional demons. I'll lose my temper over the phone.

But I've jumped through every hoop you've required of me to see June-Bug. My reward has been phone calls unanswered and not returned. Visitation that I've shown up for only to find that you or your proxy couldn't make it, or that my daughter was sleeping or wanted to go on a playdate, or a bunch of other excuses. I now regret not listening to my attorney and having visitation supervised not by friends or family but by a social worker appointed by the court. That is on me for trusting you.

However, you've reached a new low. When my attorney told me that your attorney would speak to the judge about dropping the charges if I signed my parental rights away and agreed never to speak to you or attempt contact with June, I saw red. But then I broke. I went numb. I agreed and signed the papers.

You and I both know the police report is bullshit. I have never called once at midnight demanding you wake our child so I can speak to her while drunk. Much less "calling off the hook." Nor have I shown up "at your door" in violation of the protective order. I have phone records and witnesses. But that won't matter. I'm a vet. Physically and mentally broken. That's all the court will see.

I cannot be a father if you will not let me be one. And I sure as hell cannot be one behind bars or if I decide to one day to gargle some shotgun mouthwash. So, you win. There is no way I can win, and my only option is not even a negotiated surrender but total capitulation to you.

I hope, for June-Bug's sake, that you let some light into your dark heart. As for me, I'm going to try and fix myself.

Good-bye,
Neil

Lillian grinned warmly as she re-read it. Most of the letter was pure delusion on his part. The projection and suicidal ideation right before admitting utter defeat made it obvious. The posturing about phone records and witnesses had been the flailing of his dying male ego. Deep down, Neil realized that he could not defeat her when she held the moral high ground. This is why she kept the box and its contents. It countered every moment of doubt about leaving that man in the dustbin of her history.

Lillian then undertook the familiar ritual of placing the letter on the bottom to await when it would be needed again, burying it under the weight of mementos representing what led to it. She then returned the picture to its place on top and closed the lid.

§

June heard the back door open and looked up to see her mother marching across the lawn. She noticed her mother was barefoot.

"Mom, where are your shoes? You hate walking barefoot on the grass."

"No, I just don't like this grass. It's itchy and uncomfortable. I don't understand how you can just lay on it in a bikini without a towel."

"It feels good to me."

She watched as Lillian shook her head.

"I can tell you're in a defiant mood today. Never mind, it can wait."

June sat up. "What are you talking about? You know I love it out here, and that … includes how the grass feels? I'm not being defiant, just being honest."

"No. It's more than that. Whenever you're out here, it seems like you want a fight."

"Mom, I don't want to fight. Let's talk. If you'll watch Mikey for me, I'll go get you a towel and your flip-flops. We can sit while he works off some more energy."

"It's not just that, June. It's fucking hot out here. I don't know how you can handle this blistering heat."

"Well, do you want to change into a bathing suit?"

"Look at the clouds. We've got rain coming in, probably be here as I'm walking back out the door."

"Fine," June surrendered as she watched her mother do a quick about-face. "Let me corral Mikey and we'll be right in," she said to her mother's back as the other woman practically raced to the house.

§

"Okay, Mom, what's so damn important you had to ruin your grandson's afternoon?" June said entering the kitchen. After leaving The Circle, she felt herself become irritated at her mother's commanding selfishness. She noticed a cup of tea on the table. "Tea's a good start, but you're not going to get off that easily." June sat and took a sip.

"I'm sorry, dear. I was in the basement and thinking about dinner with Charlie the other night."

June noticed Lillian's tone had softened. "Are you going to tell me about him?"

"No," Lillian said, sitting down with the cup of tea she just poured for herself. "I know all the arguments. I've had them with myself. But at the end of the day, you just don't know him like I do. You have to trust me that while this is a path you may want to go down, you will regret not listening to me."

June calmed a little as she felt her mother's hand on her arm. "I'm an adult now. I've handled my fair share of pain and disappointment."

"I know. I know. But this is different. This is the pain of a failed parent. Do you know how many kids I've pulled away from the brink of death or called their death because a parent failed them? It's not pretty when they come in with the needle they overdosed with still in their arm. Or their wrists slashed."

June lowered her eyes, staring at the tattoo that covered her own scars.

"Don't you think that was a little low?"

Lillian squeezed her arm. "Yes, but I didn't savor pushing that button. I just want you to know the stakes. The fear I feel when I think of that man letting you down again. He's hurt you enough, and you barely remember him."

June looked up and saw a tear slide down her mom's cheek. "Mom, you don't have to worry. I'm not going to do that again. I hurt myself after I found out about the other woman, but I immediately got over it. I even made a promise to Mikey—"

"You told Mikey about your cutting?" Lillian sat upright in her chair, withdrawing her touch from June.

"Yes and no. I told him in his sleep. What kind of fool or monster do you think I am?" June straightened herself in her chair, looking at her mother angrily.

Lillian's eyes locked on her, yet June did not flinch. She met the stare with resolve until her mother blinked.

"I don't think you're a monster," Lillian quickly added, "or a fool."

"Then why don't you trust me?"

"Because you keep pushing the issue. You won't let it just stay buried even though I know for a fact the past is where it needs to remain. Wisdom is trusting in the decisions of your elders."

"Oh, cut the crap, Mother," June scoffed. "Wisdom also comes from experiences. Failure is the best teacher. See, I can fling around smart-sounding slogans, too!"

"See what I said about you being defiant? Here you are! This is what I was talking about!" Lillian shook her head in exhaustion. "You're not going to let this go, are you?"

"Probably not."

"Whatever you do, just know you won't have my blessing much less my help."

IV

June pulled off I-49 and made a left crossing the overpass toward town. She coasted to the nearest pump at the Mobil station on a fume and a prayer. She checked her phone, hoping that Robert had transferred child support as promised.

"Thank God," she muttered and swung the door open, almost banging it into the concrete guard.

She slid the pump into the filler tube. The prices blinked, and she reminisced about the Quarantine of '20 when gas dropped to $1.40. Once things returned to normal, so did the high price of gas. She smiled as she pressed the button for Regular. Robert insisted on putting Premium into the Charger, but what was a single mom to do? Gloating to herself, she leaned against the dust-covered car.

"June?" The familiar voice June had been avoiding invaded the moment of self-satisfaction.

"Gerica!"

A near copy of five-year-old Gerica trundled behind her mother. A newborn dozed in a front baby carrier. The gas pump clicked off unnoticed.

"I haven't seen you since the wedding!" June said awkwardly.

Gerica's expression became serious. "I heard what Robert did to you. Shameful."

"Shameful, Mommy!" Gerica's clone exclaimed.

"Hush, child. Let me talk to Aunt June. Why don't you have a seat?" She pointed to the platform the pump sat on. "Kids, right? Speaking of, how's Mikey? Is he settling in all right? I'm sure Dr. Lillian is spoiling him."

June shook her head. "You know it. He's growing like a weed. Can't believe he's already four."

Gerica leaned in to whisper conspiratorially. "Is he, you know, seeing the deer?"

June shook her head non-committedly. "I don't know. He hasn't really talked about it."

"Have you seen the deer?"

She looked at her old friend with pleading eyes. A moment of quiet awkwardness passed between them.

"So," June broke it first, "does Nick miss the Air Force?"

"Not at all. Before he got out of active duty, he talked to an Air National Guard recruiter last year, and he enlisted and started going to drills at Saint Joe about three months ago. Once he finishes his degree, they're talking about making him a pilot." She briefly paused for a breath. "Say, are you going after that history degree you always talked about? Or was it archeology?"

"I always dreamed of doing both, but—"

"Dr. Lillian."

June smiled and nodded as Gerica switched gears.

"Hey, Grandpa told me that he had dinner with you guys. Said it was good and Michael's cooking was amazing as always. He said you looked good, but I could tell something weighed on his mind."

An amorphous male figure took shape in June's mind at the discussion of dinner. The same figure that had invaded her thoughts for years, only a slight improvement over the giant sperm inspired by her mother's epithet. June did not realize her friend had stopped talking until Gerica snapped her fingers.

"Hey, you all right? You're suddenly a thousand miles away."

"Oh, it's nothing."

"You know what," she dropped the subject, "you should come to my book club. We're reading *Carrie*, and next Friday we're going to watch the movie and drink some wine. I'm hosting. And it's Nick's drill weekend, so you'll have a place to crash."

"I don't know if I'll be able to fit in a novel with all my homework."

Gerica dismissed the objection with a wave of her hand. "We pick books that've been made into movies. A couple of the girls don't read. Besides, book club is just a polite way of saying wine club. It'll be a squad reunion: Alanna, Emily, and Hannah." She paused, considering something. "Well, I should've asked, how's the chronic fatigue? Is it bothering you still?"

"It's better. You know what, a squad reunion sounds good. Let me check with Mom and Dad to see if they can watch Mikey."

"If not, bring him! Hannah brings Riley, and the girls have a playdate. I don't think they'd mind a boy. Right, Sophia?"

Her daughter stuck her tongue out and blew a raspberry at the idea. The two mothers laughed.

"You know what, that sounds good. I'll be there."

Gerica squealed with delight before hugging her friend. "Tell Dr. Lillian hi for me and give your daddy a hug! C'mon, Sophia."

June took a moment to watch her friend walk back to her truck. A smile crept across her face. She enjoyed being home and around the people she grew up with. She turned to get in the car, almost forgetting the pump was still in the tank. Blushing at her near oversight, she replaced the pump, screwed on the cap, and slapped the fuel door shut. She had a stop to make before going home.

§

June knocked on Grandpa Charlie's door and waited for him to peek out of the curtains covering the front door's sidelights and let her in.

"June-Bug! What're you doing here?" He stepped to the side. "Come in. I just made some sun tea. You still like it sweet?"

She laughed softly. "I'd love some. Don't know if you can make it sweet enough for me, especially since I've spent the past three years in the South." She followed him into the kitchen and noticed an AR-15 laid field-stripped on the table. "Got a new toy?"

"Yep, Sarah's husband finally talked me into getting the ugly thing for the coyote pack messing with my cattle." He picked up the lower receiver. "Where's the wood? Looks like something out of *Star Trek*." He put it down and went to pour their tea. "Gerica said she bumped into you. That's good."

"Yeah, we're going to have a girls' night reunion soon."

She took the glass he offered her and sipped.

"Sweet enough?"

She smiled. "Yeah, you always had a sweet tooth." She stared at him, and he held her gaze.

"I take it you didn't come here to talk about my granddaughter or hear about my ranch issues."

"Well, we are running low on beef, so maybe I came by to see when you're going to have another cow for sale!"

He chuckled. "I've got some I put on the corn last month, so soon. But that's not why you came."

"How do you know?"

"Because your folks already bought one of them."

"Oh."

She looked at her fingers, gathering her courage. As much as she was driven to know about her father, the taboo surrounding him was so strong she felt like

53

she was pounding on a door that would remain forever locked to her.

"You want to know about your biological father."

"Is that so wrong?" Her will began to weaken as she looked at the floor. She felt as if she were sneaking behind her mother's back—betraying the woman who not only gave her life but a home to return to when her life crumbled.

"No, June-Bug. It isn't." He sighed. "Look, I love your mother and you like my own kin. I haven't been around him much, but I consider Mikey my third great-grandchild. I have my own thoughts on this, but it's not my place or story to tell. This is between you and your momma."

Her shoulders slumped. "Can't you tell me any-thing?"

"I'm surprised you haven't looked this up yourself using the Googles."

"I haven't wanted to go behind Mom's back, but I'm getting to the point where I can't let it go. I need to know."

"Between you, me, and the walls, I agree with you. I've told your momma as much. But it's not my story, so I'm not going to tell it. I've said my piece and counted to three."

She sipped her tea and looked at him thoughtfully. "So, nothing?"

"No, June-Bug. You're not going to get anything about Lillian and Neil's marriage."

"Neil?" Her lips curled into a smile.

Charlie tilted his head as if reading her grin. "Shit. You didn't even know his name?"

She shook her head.

"You're not going to tell her I slipped, are you?"

She considered the development. "Look, Grandpa Charlie, you gave me a little bit. Just give me a little more, and I'll keep this just between us."

He chuckled. "I see your mother in you. What do you want?"

"I see your mother in you ..."

"You gave me a first name. What about a last name?" She held her breath as he closed his eyes and considered her request.

"Vincent."

"Where's he from?"

"June-Bug, that wasn't part of the agreement."

"Can't blame a girl for trying." She saluted him with her glass of tea.

"No, no, I can't," he said, clinking her glass with his.

V

June felt a momentary pang of guilt as she left Mikey behind. Her rational mind justified the girls' night: Mikey got time with his grandfather and would get a mom who felt recharged in the morning—a process that began as she drove to Gerica's house on the other side of town. With her windows down, the warm breeze brought a smile to her face. In Missouri, one could get a taste of all the seasons without the extreme heat of Georgia or the brutal winters of the Upper Midwest. It helped with the guilt.

A 6:30 p.m. trip on a beautiful August Friday from her Atlanta suburb to another could be a trek often measured in hours. In Junction Falls, she made it through the business district in two minutes. Main Street ended in a fork, and she made the right. She passed the ruins of Osborne Iron Works furnace, the historical landmark's fires cool since 1893.

She next passed the abandoned, rotting Holtzer House. She tried convincing herself the momentary darkness resulted from a cloud passing in front of the sun, but she knew something inhabited the ruin. As teenagers, she and the same friends she was soon re-uniting with attempted a sleepover there—around 3:00 a.m., June had run screaming from the house and her friends followed. Having met whatever walked its aban-doned rooms, she knew it had the power to darken the day. As she cleared the property line of the home, the sun returned to the sky, her gut loosened, and the nau-sea abated. She let out a sigh of relief and accelerated.

§

The sizzle of the steaks mingled with a symphony of crickets and frogs serenading the reunion. Gerica had only thawed three steaks since Hannah and Alanna said they had other plans when invited, leaving just the best friends' triangle.

Emily was the oddball of the squad. Career-fo-cused, she moved away to attend the Missouri School of Journalism. She originally planned on becoming an anchor before discovering a taste for written journal-ism. Upon graduation, the local paper had an opening for a full-time reporter who could help the paper tran-sition online. Her only other offer? A Kansas City pa-per's society section.

"How's the new job?" June asked.

"It's going. It's not *The Missouri Times* or even *The Atlanta Journal-Constitution*, but I'm not sure they're where the future for print journalism is. Working for *The Beacon* will help me cut my teeth in digital media. I'd really like to have my own platform someday. The byline isn't the most prestigious, but it—"

"Any men in your picture, June?" Gerica interrupted, clearly bored already.

June could not tell if Emily was annoyed with her eyes hidden behind the black lenses of large round sunglasses.

"Gerica, she just got back to town!" Emily chided. "She's got a kid and is starting at a new school. I doubt she's had time to trawl Uncle Glenn's Pub or the Village Tavern for guys. Besides, it's not like they are the only option," Emily finished with a wink.

Gerica looked up from the grill with a puzzled expression. "But June's not Catholic?"

This brought an uproar of laughter from June and Emily.

"Em's suggesting I'm bi like her," June managed between laughs.

"Oh!"

"I'm just saying," Emily concluded, staring at June over her glass.

June shuffled uncomfortably in her chair and poured herself what little was left in the bottle—a perfect excuse to change the subject. "Okay, ladies, what's next? Grigio? Riesling? Merlot?"

"Why not let the guest of honor decide? What do you want?" Gerica suggested.

"Let's open the Riesling."

"You still haven't answered my question about men," Gerica pressed.

"Et tu, Gerica? It's bad enough Mom is all over it with this new therapist at the hospital."

"Has she made you an appointment yet?" Emily followed up.

"No, but it won't surprise me if she does."

"Is he cute? Wouldn't that be unethical?" Gerica asked.

"Please, we all know ethics are relative to *Doctor* Lillian Reuter, *MD*, when it comes to her family."

Emily's sarcasm brought a smile to June's face.

"Doctors aren't supposed to diagnose and treat their family, but how many times did Doctor Lillian bring home meds to shove down your throat?"

"That's different." June's tone lost its jovialness. "That's because I have myalgic encephalomyelitis."

"Yes, yes, your famous ME. What was its less technical term? Chronic fatigue syndrome or something?"

June looked away as her friend leaned toward her from across the table.

"The reason you constantly got out of gym? Or had to drop cheerleading? Or any of the other stuff you missed out on because you got worn out so easily? It kept you close to Doctor Mommy."

"Emily! I invited y'all over to have fun and welcome June home," Gerica pleaded.

"It's okay. Emily's always been direct." June looked at Gerica. "How are the steaks?"

"About done."

June could feel Emily ruminating over pressing the subject or dropping it. The other woman's internal conflict radiated like a hot stove on a summer's day. Of all her friends, Emily had been the one to clash with Lillian. When she had first been diagnosed with the disease, Emily's probing questions put her friend in the negative column of her mother's mental ledger.

A gentle touch roused June from her thoughts.

"Listen, I'm sorry. It's from a place of concern and worry. It always bugged me. Especially seeing your Insta posts at college. You were staying up late and living life. You stopped posting about ME or CFS or whatever you're calling it today."

"She's gotta point," Gerica interjected. "Now that you're home, how do you feel?"

June squirmed. "Fine. A little tired, but I'm suddenly a single mom finishing college and going through a divorce. Shouldn't I be a little tired?"

"Of course, you should be," Emily confirmed. "I couldn't imagine being in your shoes. Maybe you should ask Doc—"

June shot Emily a warning look that stopped her mid-sentence.

"—your mom to make you some tea?"

"Remember the sleepover at the Holtzer House and the basement challenge?" Gerica blurted.

June felt her muscles tense at the memory. "I appreciate the change of subject, but you could've picked a better topic."

"What? I mean it was creepy, but we were teenagers freaking each other out. It was fun!"

"Gerica, honey, you know June is our very own psychic. She just doesn't want to admit it yet."

June leaned back in her seat. "Look, I've had some experiences. And yes, I think there is more to our reality than we can dream of, but I don't think I have 'psychic powers.'"

"Maybe you should call one of those paranormal investigation shows and see if a psychic sees the same things you do," Gerica suggested. "You know, to confirm."

"I'm not a psychic. I just live in a haunted house. People don't have to be psychic to experience ghosts. I do love those shows, though." She sipped her sweet white wine. "Gerica, remember that sleepover when you said you thought you saw Mom working in her office? You distinctly saw a woman in there, but when you looked again, she was gone. And then you heard my mom snoring upstairs?"

Gerica blushed. "Point taken. But you could still find out."

"Ladies!" Emily interrupted. "There's another option."

"Aunt Sara-Lyn?" June asked.

"Aunt Sara-Lyn," Emily responded.

"Oh yeah! I forgot about her," Gerica said.

June looked away as she struggled to come up with an excuse. "That's some Ouija board, talking-to-ghosts level shit. If my dad found out, he'd lose his mind. He'd say your aunt is the devil. You know what he calls her."

"The Witch of Endor," Emily scoffed. "Listen, I get it. Your parents wouldn't like it. Michael will yell about Satan, and Doctor Lillian will go off about science and say that it's all some sort of manifestation of mental illness. She'll schedule you to be tested for bipolar disorder, schizophrenia, or whatever new illness Big Pharma is pushing a cure for."

"Either way, you end up back in the nuthouse," Gerica interjected.

The careless comment uttered from tipsy lips seemed to silence even the crickets and frogs.

"Oh shit, I'm sorry! I need to slow down on the wine," she apologized.

June held up her hand. "It's okay. You're not wrong."

"As long as we're on the topic of uncomfortable topics in our friend's life, have you asked your mom about telling you about your real dad?" Emily pushed.

"Way to throttle back," June chuckled. "It's come up, but Mom thinks it best that he remains in the past."

"That's bullshit. You're a grown woman now. If you want to know, you have that right."

"That's true, Emily," Gerica interjected from the grill, "but what if it's for the best? The guy has always sounded like such a creep."

"Sure, there's a strong probability," Emily replied. "However, if that's what we already think about June's sperm donor, what's the danger in confirming it?"

"But as it stands, June can hope her biological dad is a good guy. So if it's proven that he's not, she loses something, don't you think?"

"True, but what if everything we've ever heard about this guy is wrong? June could be missing out on a fantastic second father. It's not like she's a child anymore. She's not powerless." Emily shrugged and took a sip of wine. "Besides, with two friends like us supporting her, she'll be just fine."

June let out a chuckle.

"What's so funny?" Gerica asked.

"Nothing ... except I've had this exact fight inside my mind a thousand times. I've always imagined you two making the arguments you've just made."

"You know we're here for you. Whatever you want." Emily laid a gentle hand on June's arm. "You know you don't have to rely on just your mom. You have other resources. I can help you. Put my mad investigative skills to use."

"Hey, Gerica, how're the steaks coming?" June shouted, not so subtly changing the subject again.

"Almost there, ladies!"

§

June lay awake in Gerica's only guest bed, Emily softly snoring beside her, and thought about what she had always wanted: a happy, quiet suburban life somewhere away from Junction Falls but not as busy as a city. She thought Robert was the one who would give her all she wanted for the rest of their lives. June thought he was different, but the realization that he was just as philandering as every other boy and man she'd dated left her feeling done with relationships.

"June!" Gerica's voice snapped her out of her wandering thoughts. "June, please wake up!" Gerica began lightly shaking June.

Her voice sounded far away.

"We have to go! It's my grandpa."

June's fog cleared, and she saw the moonlight reflected in the tears of her friend. "Gerica, what happened?" she asked as she sat up in bed.

Emily stirred but did not wake beside her.

"I got a call from my mom. There was a break-in. I don't know what happened. Mom was talking fast. I heard something about a shooting and a heart attack." Gerica's voice was rapid-fire, full of dread and fear. "I need to get to the hospital and damn it, we've all been drinking!" she cried as she paced the floor in wide, lopping steps, arms crossed around her chest as she chewed at a thumbnail. "She said I needed to step on it."

June wiped at her eyes as she sat up in bed, her mind taking a moment to come up with the obvious answer. "I'll call Michael. Maybe he can come pick us up."

Gerica did not speak, only tearfully nodded.

VI

Smoke wafted from the barrel of Charlie's gun. He was out protecting a newborn calf from a pack of coyotes that had been prowling the area. His thoughts about aesthetics aside, the rifle had proved a useful tool. He dropped the magazine from his AR-15, cleared the round from the chamber, and let the bolt carrier slam forward. He replaced the unfired round in the mag and slapped it back in place for the ride back to his house.

At 9:51 p.m., night had chased all illumination from the late August sky. It had been a long day taking care of the cattle. After a shower to wash away the sweat and grime of the day, he was ready for bed. Lillian and June's being at odds weighed heavily on his mind.

"I wish you were here, Jesse," he spoke to his wife's memory. "I don't know why Lilly-Pad is so set against telling June-Bug what she wants to know. Maybe you could let me know. I talked to Sarah, but she didn't

66

want to talk about it. And I'm not going to saddle Gerica with it."

Some nights talking to Jesse led to an epiphany. Not tonight. Tonight, his beloved provided no answer. He settled into bed, immediately falling into a deep sleep.

§

Shattering glass roused Charlie. Back in '72, the Marines drafted him. The redundant and tedious drills of basic training and numerous field exercises had deeply ingrained muscle reflexes into his subconscious. The sound, loud as a gunshot in the empty house, brought him to immediate wakefulness. He was out of bed with the quickness of an active man, joints popping in protest as the only indication of age.

Rifle in hand, he found a corner with a good sightline on his locked bedroom door. His left hand rested on the charging handle as he trained the barrel on the fatal funnel. His heart pounded as his ears listened for the slightest noise.

The wood floor, unchanged from 1988, creaked on the other side of the door.

"I've got a gun!"

"Sure, old man," a cocky voice answered. "Just give me all the jewelry and any cash, and no one's gonna get hurt."

"I said leave!" Charlie chambered a round.

The other man slammed through the hollow interior door. The wood splintered in a violent rain. Charlie fired at the shadowy shape, missing his mark by less than an inch.

"Fuck!" the shape yelled and jumped backward.

Charlie's follow-up shot hit the invader square in the chest, causing him to scream and fall to the ground. Charlie saw him scramble to his feet and flee. He followed the intruder to the front door to ensure he left.

Charlie saw the taillights of a getaway car and two shadows waiting. The burglar opened the rear passenger door and climbed inside. Not knowing if he was going for a gun or leaving, Charlie shouldered the rifle and squeezed off three rounds. One hit the taillight as the driver sped off.

He retreated into his house to call 911, retrieving some TUMS from his nightstand as he dialed the three numbers.

"911, what is your emergency?" the tinny voice squeaked.

"Someone just broke into my house. I shot at him, and I think I hit him."

"Where's the suspect?"

"He fled. Two guys in a car were waiting for him and took off." His breathing was heavy from the exertion and stress of the ordeal.

"Are you still in your house? And are you safe?"

"I'm and I think so. I'm pretty sure they left."

"Police are on their way, and I'm going to stay on the line with you. Do you want me to dispatch an ambulance, too?"

"No, I think I'm—" As he started to turn down the EMTs, a sudden pain gripped his chest. The squeezing pressure dropped him to his knees. "I-I think I'm having a heart attack," he croaked, as he collapsed on the floor.

§

"Which one is it, Greg?" Lillian asked the on-duty trauma nurse as she ran toward the sound of an ambulance pulling up to the ER entrance. "The heart attack or the gunshot?"

"The gunshot, Doctor."

"Where was he shot?" She put on a surgical gown, followed by latex gloves.

"Abdomen."

She cursed in her mind. "Do we know anything more?"

"No, ma'am," the nurse replied. "Someone abandoned the patient at Higgin's Gas—"

"Got it," Lillian cut him off as the automatic doors opened and the ambulance crew rushed inside with the gurney.

"We got the bleeding under control. We think. Single GSW," the paramedic said as he kept pressure on the wound. "His BP is stabilized. He was not shot where we picked him up. He has an entry and exit wound."

Lillian appreciated the familiar paramedic who understood she took in information quickly and expected efficient reporting.

"It ruptured his intestines but appears to have missed the other organs."

She nodded, curious about the whereabouts of the on-call trauma surgeon. "Greg, is Dr. Sutton available?"

"He stepped out. His daughter is babysitting and needed something. He asked if anything came over the scanner. We said no, so he headed out to check on her. He's on his way back."

"Fuck."

The EMTs wheeled the gurney into a trauma room, freshly set up to treat a gunshot.

"I want ampicillin." She inspected the wound. "Fuck. It's a rifle shot. He's going to need a resection. How far out is Sutton?"

"About 15 minutes."

"Scalpel."

§

Seventeen minutes later, Dr. Sutton rushed into the trauma room and took over for Lillian. Other EMTs wheeled the heart attack victim into the next room. A nurse assisted her in the removal of her gloves, gown, face shield, and mask. With practiced speed and thoroughness, she washed her hands and forearms. She was used to being either the only doctor or one of two on the night shift. Most nights were slow, but busy nights were insane.

"White male, age 70," another paramedic briefed Lillian. "His house was being robbed, and he claimed to have shot the intruder."

She rolled her eyes at the extraneous information.

"He started having chest pains while on the phone with 911."

She pulled the curtain back to reveal her best friend's father. Her breath caught in her throat. "Charlie!"

It never got any easier seeing the people in her life in her ER. She tried to smile as she put the pieces of the two cases together.

"Fancy meeting you here." He smiled at her.

"Well, the good news is," she said as she studied his chart, "you're just having a little heart failure." She smiled and tried her best not to show her own worry. "We're going to order a few meds and schedule a couple of tests."

Keeping him calm was vital to give the clot-busting meds time to work, along with the other medication to lower his blood pressure and lessen the stress on his heart.

"Thank you, Lilly-Pad. You got a moment?"

"I do." She took a seat on the corner of his bed. "What's up?"

"Did they bring the boy in here? The one I shot?"

She looked away. "You know I can't say—"

He sat up in his bed and put his hand on hers. "Lillian. Look at me."

Reluctantly she did, his voice full of the firm parental authority she recalled from her childhood. His eyes welled with tears.

"Do everything you can to save that boy. I was defending myself. I don't want him to die."

"We will," Lillian whispered. She stood, slipped her hand from his, and made her notations on his chart before handing it to a nurse.

She needed a coffee and to collect herself. In the moment, it was easy. When the situation passed, she had no choice but to think about what she had just dealt with. In one room, a man she thought of as a second father fought for his life. The other housed a kid a few years younger than June. The coffee decanter was almost empty.

She closed her eyes and took a deep breath. "It's not right," she mumbled under her breath.

An ER doctor saw many injustices, and this was not the first time for her. Two months prior, a trucker fell asleep and drifted into another lane killing a young man on his way to work. The trucker survived with relatively minor injuries. But this was worse than an accident. This was pure injustice.

"Lillian?" a familiar voice said behind her, causing her to turn around.

She saw Sarah standing there clutching her purse. "How's Dad?"

Lillian forced a smile to her lips. "He's going to be just fine, just a little cardiac episode." She softened the medical speak.

"Are you sure? That makes it sound like it wasn't a heart attack."

Even as an experienced ER physician, it was almost impossible to maintain a professional distance any time a friend or family member came in.

"It is—was a heart attack, but he caught it in time. And the dispatcher had him pop an aspirin, which probably saved his life. He's a strong man. He'll make it."

"Promise?" A tear slid down Sarah's cheek. "I'm not ready to lose my other parent." She took out a tissue and dabbed her face.

"Sarah, I can only promise that I will do everything in my power to make sure Charlie walks out of this hospital as soon as possible."

"Can I see him?" Sarah asked.

"Sure, I just left him. Follow me."

§

Lillian returned to the coffee pot a few moments later to find someone had hit brew. Her thoughts drifted to her friend and the hell she and her family were going through. She had gone through that the night her parents died. She felt the anger of their untimely passing rising, mixed with the injustice of drunk drivers and home invaders living when their victims often died.

The public address system crackled to life, interrupting her thoughts. "Code Blue, Trauma 2. Code Blue, Trauma 2."

She turned and sprinted toward the room she had left only moments ago. She burst in as two nurses were trying to save Charlie's life. One gave him CPR while the other pumped a bag valve mask.

"We have ventricular fibrillation."

His heart quivered instead of pumped. The stress of the intrusion, shooting a man, and heart failure were clearly too much. The electrical impulses to his heart had become erratic.

"What does that mean, Lillian?" Sarah screeched from the corner as a third nurse entered with a defibrillator and energized it.

"It means you need to get out of here and let us do our job!" Lillian shouted as she took the paddles and pressed them to Charlie's unconscious chest. "Clear!"

The heart rate monitor remained unchanged as she sent 200 joules into his body, causing it to jerk.

"Lillian! What's going on? Save Daddy! Please!" Sarah sobbed, backing into a corner.

"Fuck! Someone get her out of here!" Lillian ordered. "300! Clear!"

One nurse gently ushered Sarah out of the room. The nurse who brought in the defibrillator adjusted the energy setting and 300 joules went into Charlie's body. The ECG displayed a line instead of a wave.

"360!" Tears started to come to Lillian's eyes.

The nurse made the adjustment.

A MOTHER'S TORMENT

"Wake up! Damn it! Clear!" She hit Charlie with the maximum the defibrillator could deliver. His body jerked from the jolt but then lay lifeless.

"Clear!" She hit him again, a tear landing on his gray-haired chest.

Once more his body spasmed before coming to rest.

"Again!" She repeated the futile exercise.

A nurse gently put his hands on hers. "Doctor, look at his skin." His tone was gentle, but his eyes bore into hers until she glanced down.

Grandpa Charlie's skin had taken on an all too familiar—and ghastly—chalky white hue.

"He's gone."

The paddles clattered to the floor, slipping from Lillian's grip as she backed away from the table, staring at the corpse in disbelief. As her back hit the wall, she slid to the floor, and for the first time since her internship, she cried over the loss of a patient.

§

Dr. Sutton exited Trauma 1 as Lillian stepped out of Trauma 2. "Great job on the resection. He's going to live."

"Thanks." She once more leaned against a wall to compose herself.

"Difficult night?"

"Yeah. That man in there, he was like a father to me." She leaned her head back, trying to hide her ex-

75

pression and her eyes, no doubt puffy and bloodshot. "His daughter is my oldest and dearest friend."

"That's right, you grew up here. I keep forgetting. I'm sorry for your loss."

She smiled. "A lot of people don't expect Asians to be from around these parts. Not many people know my family." She sighed, thinking back to growing up and taking solace in the warm memories. "Were there a few jerks? Yes, but there were a lot more Mr. Petersons who accepted me, made me want to move back here after college and med school and give back to the community that gave me so much." She looked down at the floor as an awkward silence filled the moment.

The phone at his side vibrated. He checked it. "Shit. Gotta take this."

"No worries. I'm out in an hour and have something to take care of before leaving. See you when I get back from my conference." She watched the other physician walk away.

VII

An hour after calling the time of death for Charlie, Lillian stepped into the room of the man whose life she had saved only a short time before. Her hand trembled around the syringe in her white coat's pocket. This was not the first time she had considered murder.

There had been yet another drunk driver who killed a family of four and miraculously survived the accident and a rapist shot by his victim as he fled. She had held both of their lives in her hands. It would have been easy to dispense justice instead of mercy, but her oath to do no harm held her anger at bay each time.

The man's eyes suddenly snapped open as she approached. "Oh, hey, Doc." His speech was slurred from the loss of blood and the meth he polluted it with. "Thanks for saving my life."

She moved about the room in silence as she gathered her courage. Her gloved hand shook as she cleared the air from the syringe.

"That old fuck, why'd he have a machine gun? I thought those were illegal. Stupid redneck asshole. He should be the one going to jail. Not me."

Her anger boiled just below the surface as she listened to him make himself the victim.

"You don't know, do you?" Her voice lulled as smooth as the still waters that obscured torrents below.

"Know what?"

"Mr. Peterson is dead."

He didn't even take a beat. "Good. One less selfish elderly bastard in the world."

Lillian turned toward him with the syringe in hand. She suppressed a smile as his eyes fixed on it with a junkie's hunger.

"Is that for me?" He licked his lips causing her to softly chuckle. "The nurse told me I couldn't have any. Some bullshit about meth in my system."

Lillian stared into his eyes. If she did not do *something*, he would live and go to jail. He would drain resources while a good man rotted in the ground. Her better angels told her to turn the other cheek, but the darkness whispered that this waste had robbed Charlie—her Charlie—from turning the other cheek ever again. *Besides, he'll probably get the death penalty anyway.* She felt satisfaction as the needle slid into his IV's injection port, but then her heart thundered. She paused, considered, and started to pull the needle out.

"Please, Doc. I bet you gave some to that rich fucker. Don't be a stingy bitch."

Without another thought, she swiftly injected a lethal dose of morphine mix into his IV. The meth already in his system would make death almost certain. She watched a smile spread across his face.

"Much better. Thanks, Doc."

She took care not to prick herself as she pocketed the syringe. "Don't mention it," she said over her shoulder.

She next silenced the vital signs monitor and disabled the machine's wireless connection to the nurses' station. She watched his skin turn blue.

His expression became one of confusion. His words became disjointed.

While she had seen death come for someone before, this was the first time she took satisfaction in it.

"I did it," he whispered as his eyes flickered. "He shot me, but I did it."

Lillian sneered at his pitiful—and likely last—words. She looked up at the monitor and saw that his heartbeat had flatlined. His vile heart had stopped beating. It brought a smile to her face.

Moments later, she noticed the left side of his chest was not rising like the right—that lung had stopped working. She knew his right would go next, and then it would be just the diaphragm trying in vain to keep the body alive, pushing air to non-working lungs with a heart that would not pump. Lillian stayed to listen to the gurgle of his agonal breaths. She looked him in the eyes, now partially rolled back in his head. She wanted to spit on him but caught herself before she did. The

"Don't mention it," she said over her shoulder.

realization that the justice system would judge her as a criminal compelled her to slip out of the room before he crashed.

§

"Tough night?" a nurse asked Lillian under the glow of the hospital's emergency room sign.

"Yes." She watched in fascination as he blew a smoke ring. It grew larger as it drifted upward to the heavens. "Mind if I bum a smoke?"

He shook a cigarette out of his pack and offered it to her. She took it with a shaking hand. Before she could ask for a light, he flicked his Bic, and she puffed as he lit it for her.

"Did you know either of the guys who died tonight?"

"You can't grow up here and *not* know Mr. Peterson."

She took a long drag, closed her eyes, and let the smoke trickle from her lungs.

"What about the other guy?" he asked.

A minivan's headlights momentarily blinded them as it pulled up to the main entrance. Lillian recognized Gerica as she got out and sprinted inside. She took one last drag, her hand now steady. She snuffed it on the wall and discarded it in the butt can.

"Not at all. Thanks for the smoke."

"Anytime, Doc."

§

June turned to see a sleeping Mikey in the grip of a bad dream, squirming in his car seat. She looked down at her phone and read a text message from Gerica—they didn't make it in time. Grandpa Charlie was dead.

"He has no clue what's going on," June comment-
ed, looking back at Mikey once more.

"He just knows everyone is really sad," Michael
observed as he pulled out of the hospital parking lot.
"He's empathetic, like you."

"Thanks. And thanks for coming and getting us."

"Don't mention it. The Petersons are family."

"I can't believe he's gone."

"I'm surprised you think he's gone. I thought you
believed in ghosts."

She felt his gaze fall on her for a moment before
returning to the road. She fell silent and closed her eyes
to let the wave of anger pass over her.

"Don't try and deny it. Thank you for not flaunt-
ing it, but I know you watch that haunted house show."

"What are you trying to say, exactly?" There was a
forced flatness in her tone.

"Look, what I'm trying to say is you said Charlie
is gone. I was trying to point out that there is something after this life. We raised you to believe in God and
Heaven, and I think you do. But you've got this stub-
born belief in ghosts, too. What I'm getting at is Charlie is not gone."

She relaxed. "I thought you'd be mad about me
watching the show." She twisted the conversation away
from Charlie's death.

"I'm not happy. You know how I feel about it, but
you're a woman now and a mother. You need to decide
what's good for you to consume. Be it what you buy at

the store, to what you put in your body, to what you put in your mind and spirit."

She recognized when Michael slipped into preacher mode.

"And I need to learn to trust you and the rest of my congregation."

"I'd hug you, but—"

"I know, 'I'm driving.'"

She watched him smile. "So. Does that trust extend to other topics?" Her voice warbled with anxiety.

"You know that's your mother's call. It's not mine." His shoulders slumped in the peculiar way that meant he was deferring to her mother rather than his gut.

"But do you know him?"

"I met him once or twice when your mother would bring him home on vacation. We did not get along. I think he knew I carried a torch for Lillian."

"What else?"

He shook his head. "You're good, but you're not as good as your mother. I just said too much."

"That's more than you've ever said about him. C'mon, tell me one more thing. It'll be our secret."

"June." His voice was firm, more so than even Charlie's the last time she saw him. "You're not going to extort me. I'm not going to tell you anymore. But I'll tell you what, I'll *think* about talking to your mom."

"Thank you, Daddy!"

VIII

June watched as Mikey played on the swing set Michael had built for her when she was nine. The child giggled and sporadically broke into what June termed his happy dance.

She basked in the hot August morning sun. In the distance, a calf bellowed for his mom. Other cattle made soft mooing noises as they went about their day. The scent of freshly cut hay competing with still-warm cow patties wafted on a slight breeze. Robert never liked it here. He complained about the stink of manure, but she found it much more bearable than the city smog she had grown used to.

June dug her fingers into the earth and brought the clumped dirt to her nose. It smelled clean and fresh like potting soil, not the perpetual mold and decay of Atlanta's sod.

The sound of a twig snapping in a grove of trees drew her attention.

Mikey fell silent and stopped swinging.

"Mommy, ghost!" he squealed, jumping from the swing.

A white form moved through the copse of trees.

Knock, knock, knock.

The persistent clatter drew her attention away from Mikey and the apparition. She peered over her shoulder toward the house. *Perhaps someone's at the door?*

As she walked over to where he stood inspecting the trees, she corrected him. "No, honey. Not a ghost, a deer. And an old friend whose approach I'd recognize anywhere."

A massive albino stag emerged from the tree line. Ancient, symmetrical antlers grew on its head. Points lined the beams, getting progressively smaller as they grew farther away from the base. June had the impression the majestic creature was as wise as it was old.

"Deer?" Mikey grew still and stared in innocent awe.

Knock, knock, knock.

She ignored the sound. *This is in my head. This has always been in my head. No more white coats. No more white coats.* But she couldn't help herself. "Hello, Old Man." She approached the deer as Mikey began to pet it.

As she moved, her limbs felt limp and sluggish as if in a dream, but she approached the familiar stag. Until now, she had been the only one to see the animal. At this realization, panic flashed through her mind. *But you're not real. This is a dream. Are you one of the good ones? But this is a dream. You're not real. Mikey can't see you.*

The stag started moving away from mother and son toward the armory's side yard. She took her son's hand and followed.

"... an old friend whose approach I'd recognize anywhere."

"Where are we going, Mommy?" the boy asked, his little legs trying to keep up.

She smiled. "To a special place."

Knock, knock, knock.

The knocking got louder as she got closer to The Circle. The deer's head jerked in the direction of the noise.

"What's that noise, Mommy?"

A chill ran to her core. "You hear it, too?" *Please God, not the knocking.* "But it's daylight," she wondered aloud. *Never heard it during the day.*

She began to sweat as she realized she was not standing up. Mikey's hand was not in hers. She was on her back. Eucalyptus essential oils from a diffuser replaced the scent of fresh hay and manure. The soft bellows of calves seeking their mothers surrendered to a sound familiar in its erratic, discordant rhythm.

Knock, knock, knock.

She sat up in her bed, sheets wet from sweat. She glanced around her room. The bright red numbers of her alarm clock read 3:01 a.m. She flopped back down and stared at the white ceiling, painted blue from the moon. She tried her best to hold back tears. It had started again. As a result of the stress of the divorce and starting her first full week of school in the morning, she was sure.

"Just a dream … nothing more."

Knock, knock, knock.

The noise came from the wall, where it always came from—where it would always come from. She cried until sheer exhaustion put her to sleep.

IX

June woke to a mockingbird's song coming from the giant, old oak tree in the front yard. She gazed outside and watched the branches sway as green leaves rustled gently in the breeze. She smiled and enjoyed the peace as she opened the window and took a deep breath of the fresh country air. This time the smells were real.

The alarm clock read 6:37 a.m. She had wanted to be up right at six so as not to be late for class. She bounded out of bed for a quick shower, skipped the makeup, and got dressed in her "mom shorts," a loose long-sleeved t-shirt, and her favorite pair of flip-flops.

It had been a long time since she'd woken up for school in that room, in this house. The house had a Southern exposure with a turret feature on either side, giving it a gothic aesthetic. Her room was on the east side and received the sun first. The floor sported the original wood, refurbished by her great-grandfather.

The bathroom once served as a latrine for the officers stationed there. On the other side of her bathroom was her son's room. The room once served as her playroom, having made her the only kid in her grade to enjoy multiple rooms. She tiptoed to the door and peeked in as he slept.

Seeing Mikey safely asleep, she closed the door and glanced down the hall. There were two guest bedrooms and another bathroom to her right, also facing the front yard. To her left were her father's study and the family library, separated by a large switchback staircase. The fragrance of her father's ham and cheese omelets mingled with the strong scent of coffee lured her downstairs. She did not make a sound as she followed her nose to the first floor.

She passed the expansive room that once served as either the enlisted dining hall or the ballroom based on need. There was also the commander's office and anteroom that were now living and family rooms. While too big for the family, no one ever considered selling the home because of its history, even when a developer offered her parents just under a million dollars so he could turn it into a bed and breakfast. As she started to pass a picture of her great-grandfather, she paused and studied the man, feeling pride that her parents valued his legacy over money.

That legacy began when he enlisted in the Missouri National Guard on May 25, 1940. He fought his way across Europe and then through the Korean War. After the war, he studied divinity and earned a chaplain's commission. While he still wanted to serve his brothers in arms, he felt profound guilt for participating in the violence of war. Following in his own father's footsteps and looking over the spiritual needs of his Army family offered him atonement. In '69, he retired.

In 1971, the government decommissioned the building. In 1995, it went on the auction block, and he won with a bid of $65,100. Restoring it to its former glory while converting it to his residence became his passion, and this passion did not die when he passed. Michael was a history buff and helped with the renovations. He would listen with rapt attention to the old man's stories, and the home became the family's inheritance. They moved in when she was eight, and two years later Michael completed the renovation, fully realizing her great-grandfather's dream.

June's rumbling stomach pushed these memories aside. She followed her nose to the left toward the officer's mess and the kitchen in the back of the house. She passed the rooms that had once been used by military doctors as an office and medical suite. Now they fittingly served as her mother's home office.

The sizzle and pop of bacon frying brought her toward the kitchen. She entered the room as Michael removed the last piece from the pan before ladling yellow liquid from a bowl into the popping grease. The salty, savory scent of bacon grease overpowered anything the eggs produced. Only the sweet aroma of coffee competed with the scent. Her stomach growled in anticipation.

"Omelets, Daddy?" She suppressed a yawn.

"Of course."

The battered eggs began to bubble. He formed what he called "The Original Breakfast Burrito."

"Grab yourself some coffee. It's some of that Black Rifle CAF your mother likes."

June suppressed a grin at Michael's inability to say "Caffeinated as Fuck." She grabbed her favorite mug, covered in faded princesses, and poured herself a cup.

"Sleep well?"

She sighed, taking a seat at the small table in the corner of the room and sipping the coffee. "Yes and no. I woke up around three. Took me a while to get back to sleep."

"Please tell me it wasn't the deer again," he said.

June didn't offer a response. Instead, she silently watched him let the eggs fry for a few moments before adding a mix of ham, cheese, and scallions. The bacon grease was now seared into the eggs; the cheesy ham and onion goodness of the filling then took assured victory over the coffee for aromatic supremacy. He grabbed three plates from the cabinet, divvied up the bacon, and served the first omelet to June. He stepped back to the stovetop and scooped some milky, solidified bacon grease that he kept in a recycled spaghetti jar by the window into the pan. The congealed fat sizzled and popped as it liquified. They heard Lillian coming down the stairs, which meant the next one would be hers.

She shuffled into the room and went straight for the coffee. She wore a terry cloth robe over a white t-shirt and pink boxers. She yawned as she poured the bitter liquid into a mug with "World's Best Dr. Mom" emblazoned in red letters above a black Rod of Asclepius. She kissed June on the top of her head before sitting. "We are so glad you're home."

"Me too. Thanks again for watching Mikey."

"It's our pleasure. Right, Michael?"

Michael nodded in response as he focused on cooking.

"Did you sleep well? Any—" she paused, "issues in your old room?"

"Nope." *It's too damn early for the third degree.* June dug her heels in. "Slept like a baby."

"That's good. How did Mikey do in his new room?" Lillian pressed.

"I didn't hear him at all. I think he got a good night's sleep," June parried.

"That's wonderful. Is the ME still improving? Any signs of relapse?"

"No." *Keep it to one or two words. Don't let her draw you in.*

"See any ghosts yet?" Lillian probed.

"No." *Believe me. Believe me. Believe me.*

"That's good."

June noticed the time on the microwave. "Crap, I gotta go." She scooted out of her chair and kissed her parents as she left.

§

The odor of Bvlgari cologne greeted June as she slid into the Charger's driver's seat. Her ex liked putting on airs. The car's black leather was hot against her thighs, but after Lillian's grilling, the burning sensation brought relief.

"No, you're not going there. You promised. You promised Mikey you wouldn't do that again." She closed her eyes and clenched her fists. She relaxed as the negative energy left through her fingertips. She opened her eyes and looked down at her arm. The wispy branches of a Yoshino cherry tree with cherry blossoms in full bloom covered her scars.

Continuing the ritual, she spread her legs and pushed her shorts up just a little. The looping cursive words greeted her: "I hurt myself today, to see if I still feel ..." She pushed her shorts up a little higher and revealed the semicolon. The dangling part of the comma was the only time she did not feel the tattoo gun's needles.

She closed her eyes as the scent memory of her burning flesh triggered a jumble of various sensations. The sizzle of ash meeting her skin. Johnny Cash's soulful voice covering Trent Reznor's "Hurt." The reality of the pain, the searing pain as the cigarette left a perfect, permanent circle in her skin. Her lips mouthed the words playing in her head. June forced herself back to the here and now.

"I promised you, Mikey. I'll be damned if I go down that path again." She slipped the key into the ignition and turned, hearing the engine roar to life.

On the radio, a woman's voice read the news. "—Friday. Stephen Bancroft, the man he shot in self-defense will be buried—"

"Too early for the news. Need music." June hit "Seek" on the radio.

"—the victim of an animal attack was found alive, but—"

"Why do y'all gotta read the news at the same time?" she said to herself.

"—your kids hear you cry down the hall."

Classic country would have to do. Besides, it was a good fuck-you song.

"How do you like me now? Now that I'm on my way—"

She put the car in gear and started off.

§

Michael cleaned up after Lillian retreated upstairs to shower and get ready for the day.

"Hey there, buddy," he greeted his groggy grandson while putting the last of the plates in the dishwasher. He stood and pulled a bowl from the cabinet and poured some Cookie Crisp into it. "Sleep all right?"

"Yeah, Paw-Paw." He padded over to the chair with his booster seat and climbed in.

Michael presented the cereal to his grandson and pushed the child's chair in so he could reach the bowl. "After breakfast, we can go out and play. Would you like that?"

Mikey's face lit up. "With the white deer?"

Michael froze. He and Lillian originally thought it was just an albino deer, but they never saw it in person or on one of the several trail cams Michael deployed in the months before deer season.

Mikey's smile and excitement at the thought of the white deer fell from his face. His nostrils swelled and relaxed a few times before his face scrunched up in a toddler's version of disgust. "Why do you look scared, Paw-Paw?"

"It's-it's nothing, Mikey," Michael stammered.

Michael let the boy watch cartoons while he had his breakfast, buying himself time to think.

Lillian returned downstairs and went straight to the coffee pot. "Do you want a refill?" she asked.

"I'd love one. Thanks. My mug's by the coffee pot."

He took a seat at the table and peered into the other room; Mikey's back was to them, and he was in his own little world as Lillian took her place at the table.

"You okay?"

He met her concerned gaze. "She's seeing it again."

He watched his wife shake her head. "Not again."

"It gets worse. Mikey saw it, too."

The thud of a fork hitting the plate interrupted the kitchen's quiet.

"No."

"You're the doctor. What do you think we should do?" He looked to his wife for answers. "I'm sorry. I shouldn't put that on you. Sometimes you have to be a mother instead of a doctor."

"It's okay. And you're right. Sometimes I need to step back from one to do the other. It's just so hard not to use every skill and tool to take care of your family. I don't want to lose Mikey like we almost lost June."

He reached across the table and put a loving hand on her arm. "I don't think she's going to try to kill herself again. She has Mikey in her life. She's not going to do something that'll take her away from him forever."

"I hope you're right. Sometimes I think maybe we're too hard on her."

Michael withdrew his hand from her arm and leaned back in the chair, an annoyed look on his face. "I don't think leniency is healthy. Spiritually or mentally. It could open the door to all sorts of demonic influence."

"But—"

He silenced her with his look as he leaned forward. "Ghosts. Are. Not. Real. Lillian, this is the nonsense that led to her slitting her wrists and almost dying. Had that happened … I don't want to think about it."

"Okay, okay." She cracked a smile. "You're handsome when you're angry."

Michael took a deep breath. "Any idea how you're going to spend your day off?"

"Oh, I don't know. I may organize the basement and then take some stuff to Goodwill."

"Sounds fun." He smiled, not hearing his grandson sneak back to the TV.

X

The cold light pierced the darkness of the basement as Lillian's bare feet alighted down the stair runners. The steps let out a soft moaning creek as she made her way into what she always considered the heart of the home. Even as a child, she had loved the cool and damp concrete floor. Lillian's grandfather often told her how amazed he was at her courage; most of the men who had served in the building held a superstitious fear of the space.

As an adult, her analytical mind assumed that this praise made her love it even more. She could understand the fear of others. Numerous stories began with "I felt like I was being watched." She felt it, too, but she found herself attracted to it rather than being repulsed. It made her feel safe.

"Hello, old friend," she whispered to the darkness.

Storage racks stood like sentinels and welcomed her with silence. She had to make a decision about the sperm donor and the box of mementos. As time went on, the desire to look through the letters, mixtapes, CDs, and photos lessened, but knowing it was safely compartmentalized on a shelf in the basement provided just enough sentimentality to carry her through her bouts of nihilistic self-criticism. However, its presence clearly still caused tension.

Michael still did not understand it. He often suggested she should cleanse her past by tossing it or even burning it, believing the relationship had been so toxic that perhaps cremating the box would help with closure. She had considered both but could never bring herself to go through with either. Now with June asking about him and with Charlie—*God rest his soul*—and Michael seemingly on her daughter's side, Lillian found herself considering it once more.

She moved through the basement clutter erratically as her mind avoided making any determination. The box remained patient while she collected old clothes and toys to donate to Goodwill. The remaining flotsam and jetsam would be junked. Motivation entropy took effect as she pushed the determination about the box's fate to the back of her mind. She texted Michael to come help her carry the boxes to the car.

"Come to a decision about the box?" he asked.

"No."

"I just don't understand. It makes zero sense." Michael shook his head.

"I know, but I just can't." Lillian shrugged.

"You're sure you aren't afraid June will come down here and find it?" He looked at her, adjusting his tactics.

She had to suppress a laugh. "I'm not worried."

"Not even a little?" Michael arched his eyebrow in doubt.

"Not even a little." She picked up a box and followed him upstairs. "I may make a few stops while in town. I didn't have time to properly set up Mikey's room before they moved in, so I'd like to get some things."

"Don't you think June would want to be part of that?" he asked.

"Maybe. But sometimes it's nice to be surprised." She watched his shoulders go up and down in a shrug.

"Okay, if you say so."

XI

June watched from the passenger's seat as Emily's Honda turned off the pavement and rumbled down a dirt road. This area of Junction Falls had been part of a development in the '70s to attract the local wealthy and the eccentric from Kansas City with the means to live in the middle of the woods. The smallest lot size started at five acres.

"Aunt Sara-Lyn and Uncle Derek bought like four lots to begin with. Then, when the developer couldn't sell as many as he thought, they bought six more."

"A hundred acres? How much of this is theirs?"

"We're almost there. I'll make a right at the next fork, pass another house, and then we'll be on their property."

"Is it true your aunt runs with deer?"

Emily laughed. "No. That's just asshole poachers making fun of the hippie vegetarian who shoots back."

"She sounds like fun." June forced a smile. She had butterflies in her stomach whenever she met someone new. "What if she doesn't like me? What if she thinks I'm insane?"

Emily shook her head. "She won't. She's always wanted to meet you since the first time I told her about the things you say you've experienced."

"But what if she tells me it's all in my head?"

"June. If you weren't part of my life, I wouldn't believe in my aunt's crazy stories—I need evidence. But you tell your stories with conviction. I've also seen some stuff when I'm around you, stuff I can't explain. I believe because of you. If Sara-Lyn says you're a fake, then she's either wrong or none of this supernatural stuff exists and it's in both of your heads."

June considered, for the first time, the possibility that she was just one nut job on her way to meet another. "Are we there yet?"

"Almost. Just over this hill. And. We. Are. Here."

The Honda crested the hill. At the bottom, a tiny creek cut the boundary between wood and lawn before the land began sloping up again. Two does and a fawn fed from a feeder on the edge of the lawn by the creek. They looked up at the car, then went back to grazing.

"Wow. She lives in a three-story house?"

The home looked like a log cabin with screen doors and decks on the second and third floors. The bottom level had bay windows and a standard door.

"No, that's just an illusion since it's built into the next hill. The bottom level is a walk-in basement," Emily said as they crossed the stream and started going up-hill once more.

The road ended at the back edge of the house, and she parked right before it turned to grass.

June followed her friend to the back door, and they entered without knocking.

"Aunt Sara-Lyn? Uncle Derek?" Emily announced.

"Downstairs!" a woman's voice boomed from the floorboards.

Emily took June's hand and led her through the home. Copies of gold and platinum records lined the walls, and photos of exotic places and a motley crew of people filled in the space between records. Many were '70s and '80s musicians. Others were seemingly random people. June focused on two: a woman standing next to an elderly Native American man and the same woman sitting next to a Black man in the middle of what looked like a tropical rainforest.

"I'm sure she'll tell you all about her adventures later," Emily said, dragging June along.

Dark patterned carpet sucked the light out of the basement that seemed to serve the dual purpose of a meditation chamber and home theater. Smoke from an incense stick wafted into the air.

A lithe woman hopped up from an ancient couch and greeted them. "You must be June! I've been want-ing to meet you for a long time."

Overall, the woman did not look like what June had expected. She thought the Witch of Endor, as Mi-chael called her, would look like an old crone from a

Disney movie, but this woman had a life to her. Deep lines betrayed a skin well lived in. Her long, straight hair retained a hint of its youthful darkness despite turning fully gray. She moved with speed, purpose, and a smile on her face, and she spoke in one volume: loud. Nevertheless, she looked frail, and June did her best to ignore her shriveled right hand.

"It's okay," Sara-Lyn said. "It's a congenital defect."

"I'm sorry," June said meekly. "Did you just read my mind?"

Sara-Lyn laughed, high-pitched. "No. I've had this hand all my life. In 65 years, you get used to the various reactions people have the first time you meet them. Lemme tell you, not staring is often more obvious than actually staring."

June relaxed just a little but couldn't fully put her guard down. Her eyes darted around the basement, peering into the shadows of every corner.

"Emily has told me a lot about you," Sara-Lyn continued, casting a side eye toward her niece. "What she should've told me is that you don't like basements."

Emily shook her head. "I'm sorry I didn't get you a full background."

"Am I that obvious?" June asked.

"A little, but you're putting off so much nervous energy right now. It's blocking out so much else. Tell me, do you not like the basement where you live?"

"I hate my basement. I never go down there."

"Anything traumatic ever happen to you down there?"

"No. I just never liked the place. I could count on one hand the times that I've gone down those stairs by myself."

Sara-Lyn put a hand on June's crossed arms. "Hm. Well, that's okay. Let's head upstairs to the crystal room."

"Crystal room?" June asked, raising an eyebrow.

"Yep. I've collected many through the years. All focus on good energy. You've got to be careful when you're like us. Once the door to our abilities opens, it's not just good that wants to come through. Evil likes to sneak in. You have to be on guard."

"How do you know the difference?" Emily asked.

"For me, it's faith."

"So, you believe in God? You're a Christian?" June asked.

Sara-Lyn nodded. "I grew up Catholic. Went to Immaculate Conception Elementary School. When I was six, the nuns selected me to carry baby Jesus to the altar during midnight Mass."

"Yeah, Dad has always called you 'Perfect Sara-Lyn,'" Emily interjected.

"Well, Dale's always been a little jealous of me." Sara-Lyn looked at June. "Let me guess, the rest of the Reuters still call me the Witch of Endor?"

June looked down at the floor as they made their way up from the basement.

"It's all right. I'm used to it. I used to date Mike's brother."

June paused, shocked both that someone would

call Michael "Mike" and that this woman once dated a member of her family. "Really? Which one?"

"Stephen."

"The one who died in Vietnam?"

A cloud of buried despair flickered across Sara-Lyn's face.

"I thought you hated the military," Emily stated. "You know, being a hippie and all."

Emily's aunt twirled to face her. "I *never* hated the military or the troops. I protested the *war*." She turned to June. "I dated Stephen throughout high school before he decided to enlist our senior year. I didn't like it, but he felt it was his duty. I went to college, and he came home in a coffin."

June looked at Emily. Neither of them had a frame of reference for this. A few of their classmates had chosen the military after high school, but none had died in the line of duty. The thought of losing one of them was unthinkable.

The trio ascended the stairs to the top floor, which was dominated by an open office in the center. The walls on either side of a massive oak desk were lined with floor-to-ceiling bookshelves. June's eye was drawn to the eclectic collection. *Atlas Shrugged* was shelved next to *Steal This Book*. Peeking at her, sandwiched between a book on Korean folktales and another on Haitian voodoo, was a slender tome.

She had already begun reaching for it when she caught herself. "Um, may I?"

Sara-Lyn nodded, and June pulled out the book.

"You can borrow it if it's calling to you."

June looked at the book and briefly flipped through its pages before examining the cover: *The Soul of the Indian* by Charles Alexander Eastman. The profile of a Native American in a full headdress looked up from the bottom left corner.

Emily peeked over June's shoulder. "That's kind of an offensive title," she stated. "Is it from the '80s or something?"

"Don't let the name fool you," Sara-Lyn corrected her niece. "Eastman was born *Hakadah,* which means 'the pitiful last' in Dakota. He was later renamed *Ohiye S'a,* or 'always wins,' when he grew older. He was a physician who tended to Native Americans after the Wounded Knee Massacre in 1890. He published that book in 1911." She studied June for a moment. "It makes sense that you'd pick that book."

"Why?"

"Your home is built on Missouria land."

"Well, duh. It is in Missouri." Emily chuckled.

"No, Missouria—the tribe the state's named after. I've wanted to visit your home for a long time," Sara-Lyn said.

"Oh, why?"

"I think your home is special. Not the building itself but the land. I don't want to get into my personal theories about ley lines and nexuses—yet. But your home has a history. First, it was a military armory, and a lot of people passed through there during wartime. That's going to leave a psychic mark. Then there are all the people who died there: soldiers dying in accidents, I heard a woman was murdered there, the original white settlers had their homestead burned to the ground by Jayhawkers during the Civil War, and also there was the tribe that once lived there."

"What happened to them?" June asked.

"Probably got moved to some reservation somewhere," Emily offered.

"In the 1820s, they got hit with smallpox, and that nearly wiped out the Missouria. The few who survived rejoined the Otoe tribe, which was the tribe the Missouria originally branched out from." Sara-Lyn stared at June. "Local legend has it that a group of elders who were sick opted to stay and die rather than burden the younger, healthy members of the tribe."

Emily sighed. "Great, now you're going to tell June that she's haunted by vengeful spirits from an Indian burial ground."

Sara-Lyn took off her glasses and stared at Emily. "I'm not saying anything like that. This isn't some Hollywood trope. It's history, and the tragedies and wrongs of the past echo through history." She turned her attention to June. "Not all tragedy bears poison fruit. Nobility in the face of death can echo positive energy through time and space."

"How does that even make sense?" June asked.

"Think about space as a fixed point." Sara-Lyn held her palm up and placed the index finger from her smaller hand in the middle. "You are here. What if all of time from beginning to end was happening at the exact same time? We just experience it in terms of the seconds, minutes, and hours of our lives."

Emily huffed. "I've heard this all before."

"I know your mom thinks I'm crazy and did too many drugs when I was younger. Maybe I did. But I've also read a lot." Sara-Lyn made a sweeping gesture at all the books on the shelves. "This is just one small part of my library." She pulled Walter Isaacson's biography of Albert Einstein off the shelf and pointed at the genius on the cover. "He conceived of time as the fourth dimension and theorized that we could move through it. Ever hear of Heisenberg's uncertainty principle? We've seen where atoms seem to blink in and out of existence, and quantum physics is a trip, so why can't spiritual energy travel through this dimension? I think it can."

Emily already looked bored and pulled out her phone. "I've got some texts and want to see if my editor has sent me anything yet. I'll leave you two to it."

June and Sara-Lyn watched her leave.

"I love her, but she's skeptical just like anyone else. Now, I was about to show you the crystal room," Sara-Lyn said, opening the door to a room filled with decades of collected crystals.

§

Two hours later, June was in the passenger seat of Emily's car as they drove away from Sara-Lyn's house.

"Was it everything you hoped for?" Emily asked.

June smiled. "Well, at least there's one person who doesn't think I'm crazy."

"For what it's worth, Gerica and I never really thought you were. We saw some stuff being around you. Not much, but just enough to make us less than skeptical about your abilities."

"I appreciate it. Although, I always thought you two were just holding back your barbs. I was always worried about what you were saying behind my back."

"It wasn't much. Nervous, awkward teenage girl stuff."

Mentally exhausted, June watched the trees pass as the car trundled down the dirt road. "If you believe, why did you make an excuse to duck out?"

Emily sighed. "Aunt Sara-Lyn has told me that all before. She likes talking about it. At one point, I got bored. Another thing is I was feeling like a third wheel. I figured I could knock out some work while staying out of the way."

"Oh," June answered. "I appreciate that."

"I've got something for you," Emily broke the short-lived silence. "One of the work emails is from a friend who works at the courthouse. He's got a crush on me, so it cost me a date, but he's kinda cute so not too much of a sacrifice."

"Oh?"

"Adoption records. My friend has access and has fed me some leads."

"I hope you know I'm grateful."

"It's all right. It'd be a helluva lot easier if your mom was on board and would just tell you."

"I know, but I can't afford both the divorce and the legal fees to open sealed records. Well, that and it would start a war with Mom. We have to sneak around."

XII

Standing at the door to Charlie's house, Lillian watched as the taillights of the lawyer's car disappeared around the bend. In the distance, a raven could be heard cawing—something Lillian thought appropriate for the moment. Charlie's will had just been read and, as executor, it was her job to care for the house and its contents as the inheritance process worked through the bureaucracy. He selected her to avoid the drama of a family member overseeing the process; plus, he trusted her like family.

With a heavy sigh, she locked the door behind her and crossed the lawn to her car, her black heels stabbing the soft earth beneath her. The reading had been difficult. The anguished expressions on the family's faces made Lillian want to scream. She fought the urge to kick off her heels, climb onto her chair, and declare that she provided them with justice. The piece of shit that did this to Charlie and to them had died by her own hand. It took all her willpower to remain calm and impassive during the reading of the last will and testament.

Before entering her car, Lillian took a moment to observe the crime scene. She'd noticed the family had parked in the grass, not wanting to disturb the deep scars in the gravel from where the getaway car had sped off. She walked over, imagining the young man stumbling to the vehicle, clutching his wound. It brought a smile to her face.

The sunlight glinting off a red piece of what looked like plastic called her attention. She studied it for a moment before realizing it was a fragment of a taillight. As soon as she touched it, she could imagine his pained face in the backseat as the criminals sped away.

She rubbed it with her thumb, the texture reminiscent of the syringe she used to kill him. She had done well getting justice. Lillian slipped it into her purse and, after shooing a raven from her car, slid into the driver's seat, feeling contentment for the first time since Charlie's death.

XIII

The acrid fragrance of gunpowder wafted to Michael's nostrils as the crack of the last shot echoed through the valley. He leaned to his right and peeked through his spotting scope at another 0.357-inch hole punched through a picture of his former son-in-law. He then aimed at a different picture on the homemade target stand. He squeezed the trigger and put a hole through that paper target, too.

Typically, Michael was not a violent man, but he would protect his family. He grew up hunting but had never felt the need to own a handgun until Lillian returned to Junction Falls and his life. Her stories about her marriage to a former Marine with post-traumatic stress disorder filled him with dread. Neil Vincent was a man of violence. He vowed to never allow Vincent to harass his wife and adopted daughter again, so he bought the revolver. He swore such a vow once more when June's marriage failed and she called to ask if she could move back home. Unfortunately, guns could not stop his daughter's unseen demons.

The sound of Emily dropping June off stirred Michael from his meditation and signaled the end of his target practice. He swung the cylinder gate open and ejected spent brass and unfired rounds to put the firearm back in the case on the shooter's table he'd built.

"Hi, Daddy."

Her words elicited a smile from him. "How was lunch with Em?"

"All right." June shifted nervously from one foot to another. "Where's Mikey?"

Michael held up a baby monitor. "He went down for a nap about 20 minutes ago."

"The noise didn't wake him?"

"Nah, he's on the far end of the house. Plus, I was shooting .38 target loads, not the magnum rounds. A little bit quieter. The kid's a deep sleeper."

The relief his words brought to her face could not be missed.

Her eyes locked onto the case. "I'm glad to see you've still got the three-fifty-seven. I wondered if you'd sold it."

Michael chuckled. "Well, I have more hobbies than cooking and my garden." He glanced over at the small section of the yard dedicated to his herbs. "Let me—" Michael suddenly paled. "Let me p-put this away, and you can help me. I've got some sage that's ready to harvest and dry."

115

He couldn't believe his lapse. After June's suicide attempt, Lillian prohibited her access to guns.

"I started shooting again myself," June interjected.

"Oh?" Michael asked, surprised.

"Yeah. We'd head down to the riverbank and plink at cans or targets. Robert preferred semi-autos though."

He raised an eyebrow. "City boys."

"So do you have any spare ammo?"

Michael hesitated. "Your mother wouldn't approve."

"What she doesn't know can't hurt us." Her lips curled into a conspiratorial grin. "I'm not suicidal anymore. Besides," she shifted her weight awkwardly from one foot to another, "I would've never used your gun."

"Well, your mother—"

"—is a doctor and believes in an overabundance of caution. I get it. But I'm not 16 anymore."

Michael set the case back down on the shooter's table, his hand resting on the carry handle. He stared at his daughter. She was a woman now, capable of managing her own health and risk thereto. Sometimes he just still saw the little girl who stole his heart. Giving in, his own lips curled into a grin. "You still remember how to load a *real* gun?"

"It's like riding a bike, right?" She opened the case and lifted the gun. "So, what're we shooting at?" A wicked countenance spread across her face as she looked down range and saw an unpunched, 8"x10" portrait of Robert standing in his wedding tux. "Never mind."

Michael watched as she swung the cylinder gate open and loaded it with a speedloader. With a flick of her wrist, she snapped the gate closed and brought the gun to bear on her target. Sighting down the six-inch barrel, June took control of her breathing. Memories of teaching her to shoot when she was about 10 flashed through Michael's mind. Back then, he had to wrap his arms around her to steady her aim and ensure her safety.

She squeezed the trigger, punching a hole well below her ex-husband's face. "I've missed this."

Michael studied the target through the spotting scope. "You've missed your target."

"Did I?" She giggled.

It was then Michael realized the shot was placed square in Robert's crotch.

June was sighting down the barrel once more and moderating her breathing when the baby monitor sparked to life. Green LEDs lit up, and they heard the faint sound of Mikey's sleep-filled voice calling for her.

"Go. I'll clean up." Michael took the handgun from her as she relaxed her stance.

"Thanks, Daddy." She kissed him on the cheek and jogged toward the house.

§

Once Michael headed through the back door, he started to call for June. "Thank—"

"Mikey's upset! He heard you talking to Mom about ghosts. About me."

His smile fell from his face. "I'm sorry, honey." He had seen the same temper in Lillian, only June tended to suppress it more. Still, he did not like being on the receiving end. "I thought he was in the other room watching his shows."

She shook her head. "Kids hear things, you know. He heard you talking about me trying to kill myself!"

He lowered his head, unable to look at her.

"It's a miracle you got him to go to sleep!"

"June, I—"

She held up a hand. "I can't." Her shoulders slumped as her tone softened. "Just be more careful."

Father and daughter stared at each other, searching for what to say next. On cue, Mikey called for his mother.

"I've got this," June said and turned to go comfort her son.

XIV

June awoke curled around her son on the floor of her childhood playroom. Still upset from the conversation Mikey overheard, he had refused to go back to sleep until she agreed to stay with him. She intended to just stay for a quick snuggle and then sneak out and study. Instead, she had fallen asleep.

She finally slipped out after putting Mikey in his bed and tiptoed back to her room. It was time for her guilty pleasure: *Haunted Houses*, a reality show that followed a medium and his wife who investigated claims of hauntings. The show aired on the Vacation Channel since they traveled the country to help people with the supernatural. Robert found the concept silly and beneath him, which was one of the few things he and Lillian agreed on, dismissing it as unscientific. And Michael did not like the show on religious grounds. He thought such shows were a gateway to Satanism, and he "prohibited" them under his roof.

And like he said, I'm grown up now and can decide what is or isn't appropriate viewing.

Still, she scooted close to the TV, like a child watching cartoons when she should be sleeping.

§

An hour later, she turned off the TV and collected her books. The episodes brought her a sense of relief. She saw herself reflected in the people who called in for help. She did not feel alone. Sure, she had posted on some Reddit paranormal pages, but seeing real people and their homes or businesses made the stories more real. Some were obvious hoaxers or scammers—she rarely finished those episodes—but when she sensed the sincerity of the people who called in, she found emotional release.

The one part of the show she hated was the appeals the hosts made during the commercials and after the end credits: appeals for viewers to call in and share their stories. She wanted to share her experiences but feared her parents' wrath. She needed help that her mother's medicine and father's religion couldn't provide. She once more resisted the temptation to pick up the phone and call the 1-800 number listed on the screen, heading into the bathroom instead. Her visit with Sara-Lyn also reinforced her conviction not to call. A glimmer of hope had started to form around the thought that she may be able to figure this out herself.

She put her hair into a ponytail and slipped on a pair of yoga pants and a long-sleeve t-shirt. Her mother kept her study so cold, even in the summer. But when not used by Lillian, the room provided an excellent space to be productive.

At the bottom of the stairs, June noticed a soft, ethereal blue light spilling from the open doorway. She peeked in, and the cold glow of a computer screen framed her mother sitting with her back to the door. Earphones blared music from the '90s. June attempted to back out of the doorway silently, but it wasn't silently enough.

The motion caught her mother's eye, and Lillian swiveled around to face her. She wore a pained expression.

"You okay, Mom?" June asked.

"Yes, sweet pea. Just one of those cramps I get. It must be the chair."

"Didn't you bring it home from work?"

"Yes, I did. I don't spend much time sitting at work when gunshot wounds, four-wheeler accidents, and heart attacks interrupt me every five minutes."

"Still, you should go to a doctor."

"I've gone to Dr. Talbot, and he can't find anything wrong. I just cannot seem to find a decent ergonomic chair."

"Maybe it's something, or someone, in this room?" June leaned against the door frame.

"Seriously, June, not everything is because of ghosts." Lillian rubbed her eyes.

"Not *everything*? Are you saying that *some* things are caused by ghosts?"

Gotcha!

"You know what I mean." Lillian's tone was irritated, which pleased June. "Did you want to use my study?"

"Yes, but I can come back later if you're working." She dared not push her luck.

"Nonsense. You have homework. The world's economies need you to apply that creative brain of yours to its ills."

"More than the planet needs my abilities to talk to—" she started, deciding to push her luck after all.

"—your invisible friends?" Lillian finished, her expression brightening as June's dimmed. "Yes, I know you don't like it when I call them that, but we need to chat. Please, have a seat." She turned around and motioned to the chair on the other side of her desk.

"Why do I feel like I'm 10 again?"

Might as well get this over with.

"No, you are a mother now. You need to think about what you are putting into your son's mind. Your father said Mikey is talking about seeing the deer and some guy in the dining room, and don't forget about your fear of the basement. Think about your childhood. Remember how it crushed you when other kids did not believe your ghost stories?"

June fell silent for a few moments, contemplating her mother's words. She obviously knew about her son seeing the same deer she'd seen since childhood, but it was news to her that he was now seeing other spirits. It made June's blood run cold. "Mom, children can be pretty gullible." She gazed at her feet to avoid her mother's inquisitorial stare.

"I'm not talking about the other children, honey. I'm talking about you since you were a teen. You should've outgrown these fantasies." Lillian reached across her desk to her daughter.

June made the mistake of looking up so Lillian could read her face.

Lillian shook her head. "I love you, sweet pea. Your dad loves you. We don't say these things to hurt you. It's because we care and want the best for you and Mikey. We don't believe in ghosts, and I think the time has come for you to confront this obsession."

"But Mom, how do I deny what I have seen? They are real to me—not an obsession."

Lillian got up from her chair, came out from behind her desk, and hugged her daughter. "I have a new idea. It's called cognitive behavioral therapy. You need to confront your fear. I have been thinking about this for a while now." She slowly pulled back enough to stare June in the eye. "Look, I know you think there is a lot to unpack with your biological father, but because of all this, I'm not convinced that you're up to it. Plus, you're still picking yourself up from the divorce."

June couldn't believe how her mother would twist things. "Damn it, Mom! I'm a grown-up now! A mother!" She instantly regretted the tone of her voice.

"I will not be disrespected in my own home," her mother said. "This is my decision. Yes, you may have a right to know," Lillian sighed and softened her tone, "but you don't have a right to force me to talk about it until I'm damn well good and ready."

The soft tone scared June just as much now as it did when she was growing up, how the quietness of her mother's voice betrayed the rage it constrained.

"And you think you're ready?" Lillian continued. "You're so grown up? You can't even go into the basement."

"I could if I wanted."

"Please," her mother said, waiting for her to disagree.

June felt the urge to cry as her mother scoffed at her and could not bring herself to argue.

"Child, what am I going to do with you?"

"Perhaps not treat me like a child? Perhaps you could tell me a little bit at a time?"

While she and Emily conspired and still planned to solve the mystery of the sperm donor regardless, a part of her still wanted to hear it from her mother first. She watched as her mother sat down, her back straight in the chair.

"Fine." Ice dripped from the word. "What do you want to know?"

"Why did he leave? I cannot imagine leaving Mikey."

"I think we both knew the marriage wouldn't last," Lillian spat, her tone dripping with disgust and regret.

124

Her gaze shifted from holding June's eyes to an imaginary place a long time past and far away from Junction Falls. "Things were … bad." Her tone changed into one of practiced resignation. "He only cared about his career and money. I had to fight for every dime of child support I got from the court."

"What did he do for a living?"

"He was an accountant but not a very skilled one. He struggled, bouncing from job to job. Never going anywhere except the liquor store, at which point—"

"It's okay, Mom," June said, reaching for Lillian's arm to give her a supportive squeeze. "If it helps, I could reach out to him myself?"

She watched a flash of rage and fear spread across her mother's face.

"You are playing with fire, girl. I will not be the one who burns you." Lillian shook her head. "No. I forbid you from contacting him."

"But Mom—" June began to object.

"No buts. That is too much for me to deal with. I'm not ready." Her shoulders rose and fell as she sighed. She waved her hand as if dismissing an employee.

§

Heart pounding, June made her way through her darkened home. As she strode down the hallway, thoughts of the basement would not leave her at peace. She *hated* the basement. The unfinished subterranean floor oozed evil.

Maybe if I just went down there she would see I'm not a child, see that I can face my fears and the past.

She turned and started toward the basement. Her stride, defiant and resolute at first, became more hesitant as she approached the door. June closed her eyes. She knew she would lose her nerve if she saw a spirit—but she was supposed to be being brave. She forced them open and reached for the knob with a trembling hand, but her body seemed to have a mind of its own. Her hand refused to touch the antique metal. She tried closing her eyes again and willed her muscles to reach for it, half-expecting to be scalded. The antique brass was cold. June sensed the icy hate and even colder welcome from the basement.

She tried telling herself it was all her imagination, using all of the self-talk tools she'd been given in her years of therapy.

Face this silly fear from your childhood and your mother will tell you whatever you want—what you need—to know about your father.

The hairs on the back of her neck stood on end as she ventured to confront the evil presence that waited for her at the bottom of the stairs.

XV

June stepped forward into the darkness without looking, choosing to trust herself.

You can do this. You're an adult.

The ancient wooden stair creaked under her weight. She paused and opened her eyes.

That noise? Only a mouse.

Another step. Another creak.

It smells like someone opened a jar that was kept in the fridge for a week too long.

The next step was solid and issued no creak.

I'm okay. I should've done this a long time ago.

The temperature dropped as she reached the bottom of the stairs. She extended a hand and pulled a string, turning on an uncovered bulb. The faint light of the squiggle-shaped glass barely pierced the darkness; everything beyond 10 feet of the fixture remained concealed in shadow. She took a deep breath and crossed her arms over her chest, rubbing up and down to both warm herself and steel her resolve to push deeper.

"I'm the only person down here. I *am* alone. There's nothing down here to hurt me." The sound of her voice comfortably pierced the silence.

The moisture of the frigid stone floor seeped through the light synthetic fabric of her socks.

"Should've put on shoes," her voice quivered as she resisted a primal urge to panic.

A dark recess of her mind screamed for her to turn and run upstairs. She stopped and stood to calm her body. It took a moment, but her heart rate returned to something close to normal.

The gray steel frames of industrial shelving units stood in dark contrast to the off-white color of the stone walls and floor. Plastic storage tubs and banker's boxes stood silent on particleboard shelves. Most were covered with years of dust, their contents long forgotten or deemed too unimportant to be remembered but just important enough to be stored. The labels of other tubs indicating holidays like Christmas or Thanksgiving sported only a thin layer of dust.

Something brushed against her face. Startled, she jumped backward. She let out a nervous giggle when she saw the pull string of another light.

"Okay, *some* of it might just be in my head."

She pulled on the string. The faint glow illuminated a banker's box labeled "Mementos," which sported significantly less dust than its neighbors. She pulled it down to rummage through it. She discovered a faded picture and held it up so the light could reveal it. Her mother, about the same age as June was now, stood next to a man. Standing about 6' 2", the man had his arm around Lillian's shoulders and held her close as if he never wanted to be separated from her. They stood on a beach with sapphire and turquoise blue waves crashing to shore behind them. He was shirtless with a hairless, muscular chest and broad shoulders. His red hair was a stark contrast to her mother's raven locks. He looked familiar—someone embedded deep in the foggy banks of her earliest memories.

She flipped the photo over and in unfamiliar handwriting was the word "Honeymoon."

"Hello, Neil Vincent. I'm June, your daughter." June's breath caught, and she felt a tear slide down her cheek.

She quickly wiped away the tear before folding the photo and slipping it into her back pocket to look at and process later. Right now, she had the rest of the contents to rummage through. Her focus shifted to the various pictures and love letters. Several aged photographs showed a glowing and pregnant Lillian or an infant June in her biological father's arms, a look of joy on his face. She wondered what happened to that happy little family.

Slowly, her ears began to prickle, and a chill tingled up her spine as she heard what sounded like a person shuffling across the floor. She turned but saw nothing there. She fished out her cell phone and turned on its flashlight to pan feebly around the various shelves.

Nothing. She peeked through the voids between the tubs on the shelves behind her. A few times she thought the shadows stirred. Yet when the beam perforated the darkness, it revealed nothing but empty space or the skeletal outline of a shelf.

She shook her head. "Maybe Mom and Dad are right. Maybe I do have an overactive imagination." Her shoulders rose as she took a deep breath and then exhaled. "There's family archeology to be done."

She took a seat on the floor, crossing her legs under her as she flipped through the photos and read a letter or two. Some of them brought tears to her eyes. At some point, her biological parents loved each other. This was evident in the sperm donor's attempt at *sijo*, a Korean form of poetry that Lillian had taught her after she learned the Japanese haiku in the fourth grade:

How I would die a thousand deaths for my Lillian,
nae sarang,
Long after the Sun devours the Earth, and our souls
have become cosmic energy,
My love shall remain for nae sarang, and
beautiful gongjunim.

June's tears splattered on the page, smudging the ink in her father's handwriting. She felt a tug at her heart as her tears erased even this little bit of him. Next, she found a notebook. She flipped open the cover and saw her mother's handwriting. The paper bubbled in spots with ink also smeared from tears.

The letter detailed her father's bad deeds. Abuse, first against her mother and then against her. One Friday night he left, telling Lillian he was going camping with friends. He never returned. The following Friday the postman knocked on the door. He required a signature for a flat envelope with a proposed divorce agreement. This letter was written but never sent, and reading it broke June's heart. One of her tears splattered on the paper and stained it just like her mother's.

You still could've been my dad. Why didn't you want me? Why were you so mean to us? How could you be such a fuckin' ass?

She sighed heavily and replaced the notebook and other pictures save for the folded one in her back pocket. She put the lid back on the box and stood up. Again, her ears prickled as she heard the shuffling noise.

It's just my imagination.

"I'm *not* going to turn around and give you the satisfaction." She tried to convince herself.

She lifted the box and slid it back into its place on the shelf. Knowing Lillian would be furious at this invasion of privacy, she brushed the dust off the tubs on either side to make it less obvious that it had been disturbed.

Unheard, two tubs behind June moved a little as a hand pushed between them, crossing the void between shelves in a lethargic slither toward her back.

Almost done, June refused to pay attention to the hairs standing up on the back of her neck.

"It's only my imagination."

She *thought* something delicately brushed against her ponytail. She was wiping her hands on her yoga pants to get the dust off them when a finger caressed the back of her exposed neck. It was cold yet soft, flesh yielding to the hard bone beneath.

"Not funny, Mother." She forced a playful tone into her voice.

The sensation changed as the finger pressed against her exposed skin. The sharp end of bone pushing through flesh scratched her. She turned to see behind her. The faint light illuminated two tubs and disturbed dust fluttering back onto a shelf.

No one was there.

She screamed and ran upstairs to her mother.

§

Lillian was startled at hearing June's scream. Moments later the girl burst into her office with skin white as a sheet.

"Momma! Momma!" June choked. "I went downstairs! I wanted to show you how brave I am!" Her childlike tone added irony to her next words. "How grown up!"

Lillian swiveled in her chair as her child made her way to the desk. "It's okay, come here." She was surprised when June dropped to her knees and laid her head in her lap. As her ponytail slid to one side, a trickle of blood caught her eye. "Honey, you scratched yourself."

132

June looked up slowly, no longer looking the part of the scared child. She coldly met Lillian's gaze. "No, I didn't. Something *touched* me from behind. No way I brushed against something."

"What's going on in here?" Michael's sleepy voice interrupted.

"Nothing. June picked tonight to go into the basement." She could read the "I told you so" expression her husband wore. "We'll talk about it later."

"Okay."

"Still, I might sleep in her room tonight."

"Killing two birds with one stone?" he asked, as June's face melted into its previous expression of fear and she buried her head farther into Lillian's lap.

He meant she could take care of their daughter and delay admitting she was wrong.

"I don't know what you mean."

XVI

The first rays of the morning sun stirred Lillian awake as she held June. She brushed June's ponytail off her neck to once more examine the scratch. She studied a ragged dotted line of broken skin. It traced along the ridge of vertebrae just below her daughter's skull, the flesh around it an angry shade of red. She had been searching for a rational explanation ever since her daughter burst back upstairs in a panic, her imagination having run wild. She probably just brushed against one of the many sharp metal edges of the shelves they had installed in the basement. But the only thing that could calm her down was her mother holding her as she fell asleep.

As Lillian gently continued to examine the scratch, June stirred. It needed some more antibiotic ointment. She made a mental note to ask her daughter about her immunizations; she might need a tetanus shot. Once it was clear June wasn't waking up, her thoughts drifted from the physiological to the psychological.

What had June been doing down there? Did she go through any of the tubs? Did she go through *the* tub? If she had, she'd be insufferable and never stop pestering Lillian about Neil.

Neil Vincent was a man that had been deployed during Operation Desert Storm during which his back was broken and half of his leg was lost when the Humvee he was in hit an IED. Languishing for a year in a Navy hospital, Neil managed to knock out three semesters of community college. Once medically retired and receiving a VA disability, the GI Bill helped him survive as he attended Johns Hopkins University. It was there he met Lillian while she was doing her internship and residency.

They met at a bar when they were both in between relationships, and they hit it off enough to enjoy some intense break-up sex. She had apparently left an impression on him greater than her sexual prowess, resulting in him pursuing her for more than she initially wanted. He had a sensitive streak well hidden under his gruff Marine exterior.

Soon the smitten former Marine had grown on her, and they began dating. Neil had even learned how to write some bad poetry in the traditional Korean style. He called her *nae sarang*, which means "my love" in Korean. Six months later, after he graduated with his accounting degree and was studying for his CPA exam, they married. That's when his drinking became a problem. The happy-go-lucky guy she had met and reluctantly fallen in love with disappeared. He drank too much, and when he drank, he got angry. But a year later when she finished her residency, she was pregnant with June. She hoped this would save her marriage. She hoped a baby would calm him down, and it did—at first. He coined the nickname "June-Bug" and even expanded his knowledge of Korean to call her *gongjunim*, which means "princess."

But then he lost his job and struggled to find a new accounting position. He drank more, and the budget became tighter. Eventually, he swallowed his pride and took a position in the shipping department of a factory. The repetitive, physical nature of the job reignited the pain of his old injuries. He drank more, and their arguments became more intense. Increasingly, she became more afraid of his verbal and physical outbursts. He never hit her until the night he left. Lillian still physically winced at the memory.

§

Mikey stirred as he slept, his dreams of simple childhood joys and pleasures slowly turning dark. He squirmed and let out a soft whimper. A man invaded his dreams, turning them into a nightmare. He did not know this man, but he was old and had lived in his grandparents' house a long time—like the deer but not as nice. He felt the man's hand on his throat, icy and strong. Slowly it began to squeeze. The child thrashed in his bed, twisting in the sheets. He shrieked, the bone-chilling scream bouncing off the walls.

§

Although June was deep asleep and Lillian fully awake, June was still first to bolt out of bed when they heard Mikey scream. By the time Lillian made it to his bedroom, June already had her arms wrapped around his tiny body.

"What's wrong?" she asked as she entered the room.

"He just had a bad dream," June answered, rubbing Mikey's back.

"What's going on?" Michael asked as he entered.

"Mikey just had a nightmare," Lillian answered. "Let's go make pancakes while she calms him down."

§

"Where's Mom?" June asked after putting on *Star Wars Rebels* for Mikey in the living room.

"Down in the basement," Michael said, taking off a pancake and plating it. He poured the batter for the next one. "She wanted to look for something."

June took the fresh pancake, spreading butter on it before pouring the syrup. She remained silent as she settled into the kitchen's breakfast nook. She hoped she had covered her tracks well enough. If not, there would be hell to pay.

"Mikey's not joining us?"

"No, he wants to watch his show." She forked some pancake into her mouth. She almost asked if she was like that when she was four, but Michael was not the parent to ask that question. She was four when Lillian married him.

"Ah." He flipped the next flapjack. "I think I hear her coming upstairs now."

"Hey, Mom, when I was four—"

"We need to talk." She was not happy.

Michael turned and looked at his wife. "What's wrong?"

June stayed silent.

"June went through one of my memento boxes."

Michael nodded, eyes wide, and slowly turned around and went back to cooking.

June calmly took another bite. "Well, you *did* push me into exploring the basement."

"No, I encouraged you to confront your irrational fears. Not snoop."

"What's the big deal?"

"I know you want to know. You have questions." She sighed deeply. "But I don't think it's healthy for you to focus on someone who was barely in your life. The last time you set eyes on him, you were not much older than Mikey is now. He was never *really* a father to you. That's why we call him the sperm donor."

"Yes, we've had this conversation before. I know that he wasn't a good guy, and he wasn't *really* my father. That honor goes to Daddy." She tilted her head toward Michael. "But what if I inherited something from him? What if part of my personality is like his? I just want to know."

Her mother snorted. "You are *nothing* like him. Trust me."

June could feel herself getting more irritated as the conversation wore on.

§

Mikey was enjoying his favorite cartoon when he looked up.

"You're funny," he said, giggling. "I'm Mikey, Headman." He cocked his head at the strange man staring down at him. "I see the wall through you."

The apparition spoke.

"I don't know what you're saying," he said, turning his attention back to the TV.

§

"Did you hear that?" June asked, hearing her son's voice.

"Sounds like Mikey is talking to himself," Michael said, his tone calm and soothing. "He must get that from you; you used to talk to yourself when I first met you."

She smiled. Now that she was a parent, she wanted to know what quirky little things she did as a child that were now lost to the fog of memory.

"See," Lillian interrupted, "you don't need to know about some deadbeat to know your past. That's what Michael and I are for." She stepped over to the counter to get herself some pancakes. "Why dig up painful memories?"

"But, Mom, why not? Especially if I want to. Why not let me talk to him?"

"What makes you think I have any way of contacting him?"

"Do you?"

The question was plainly put to her, and she paused for a bit too long.

"You *do* know how to contact him!" June paused for an answer "Nothing? I see. I'm an adult now—a mother—but you *still* want to treat me like a child!" She pounded the table in a chimera of anger and defiance.

"I *want* to *protect* you," Lillian hissed. "He's a drunk. He's a deadbeat."

"Protect me from what? Myself? This is my decision. Is this about what happened when I was 16?"

"You mean what you *did* when you were 16?" Lillian left no time for the weight of the words to settle. "Yes! I don't want to see you get that depressed again! Hurt yourself!"

"Ladies!" Michael raised his voice.

His wife and daughter turned and looked at him.

"Do you hear that?" he asked, suddenly on edge.

"No," Lillian replied.

"I don't hear anyth—" June's voice trailed as she realized she could not even hear the TV.

They heard a thud from the living room, and June sprinted from the kitchen, toppling her chair.

She found her son unconscious on the floor.

XVII

June carried Mikey to the car.

Lillian slid next to them in the back seat. She checked his pulse and breathing. "He's just unconscious." She tried examining Mikey on the way, but he started squirming whenever she would get close to his neck.

Mother and grandmother were relieved as he regained consciousness before they pulled into the ER's ambulance entrance.

Lillian entered the hospital issuing commands. "Ajit, I need someone to put in a neurological consult and an MRI for my grandson."

"Lillian, step back and just be a grandmother," Ajit said as he began his examination. "So, tell me what happened."

June answered before Lillian could, her voice beating a staccato rhythm. "He was watching his cartoons in another room. We heard something hit the floor. We ran in and found him on the floor unconscious."

Lillian watched the other physician go through his examination, letting June handle the talking for once.

"There's a bump on the back of his head. You said you all heard a thud, right?"

"Yes, Dr. Patel," June responded.

"Okay, then you know what happened. He was probably playing on a piece of furniture and fell, knocking himself out." He tickled the boy's belly. "Now," his voice got serious, "I have questions about the marks on his neck." Gently, he lifted the boy's head by the chin. A pinkish ring ran around his neck. "Did you notice this?"

"He didn't have it this morning. I haven't seen that before." Panic rose in June's voice. "What-what could have caused that?"

Ajit looked at Lillian and Michael. "Did either one of you see him this morning? Before he was knocked unconscious?"

"I didn't," Michael answered honestly. "Well, I mean, I saw him for just a moment. He woke up screaming from a nightmare and I ran into his room, but June and Lillian were already there."

"I saw him this morning when he woke up. He didn't have it then," Lillian said.

"And you were all in the same room when he got hurt? There was no one else in the home?"

He was walking a fine line. Lillian knew what he was doing.

142

"Yes, Ajit," Lillian spoke up. "We were all together when Mikey got hurt. He was in the other room watching his cartoon. No one else was in the room. This is not abuse. You know me, my family. You know we're not capable of that."

He took a deep breath and capped his pen, sticking it in his white coat. "That I do, Lillian. And you're right, of course, but you know the policy."

She smiled. "I know, I know. But I'm telling you, none of us did this."

He chuckled. "I remember when I first started here. June seemed to always be sick or falling out of trees. Like mother, like child."

PART TWO:
Points of Know Return

Why do spirits remain after death? For many reasons. However, the most common reason, in my experience, is unfinished business. For some, this is a life goal that wasn't reached. For others, it's guilt over some sin or wrong they didn't get a chance to— or even refused to—atone for before dying.

There's this theme that recurs throughout human history and spiritualism. It's the weighing of human souls to go to a version of either Heaven or Hell. I've often wondered whether or not souls that balanced the scales remain until they can tilt them one way or another.

It is far easier to fix what we've broken in our corporeal form. Once we cross over the veil between life and death, we lose the ability to communicate and interact with the physical world. So, it's very important that we do not leave loose ends when we die. For most, death is the ultimate point of no return.

— Dick Fisher, Spirit Medium
Co-host, *Haunted Houses*

XVIII

The Post-It with her father's—a stranger's—contact information scrawled in Emily's handwriting stared at June with ominous hope. He did not have much of a social media presence, and what he did have was locked down for privacy. He had even obscured his Facebook name as "Vince Neal." Her body tingled with the anticipation that she would be able to reconnect and get the closure she desperately needed—the closure that her mother repeatedly prevented her from getting.

June's drive to discover her mystery father's secrets was only accelerated by Mikey's trip to the ER and the questions of abuse Dr. Patel had raised.

Her mother was fond of saying "When you hear hoofbeats, think horses not zebras." After being the subject of concern, she began to wonder if ER doctors were conditioned to knee-jerk allegations of abuse much like they made knee-jerk decisions that it was horses over zebras. If so, perhaps she owed this stranger an opportunity to explain himself.

She busied herself with fully setting up the Facebook account she had just created, procrastinating doing what she most wanted to do.

"It'd be so much easier and safer if you used Insta, old man," she said quietly.

It didn't feel right to call him "Dad," but "Neil" didn't feel right either.

She chose the name JL Smythe from Atlanta in hopes her mother would not stumble across the shadow account. However, her first initials with his ex-wife's maiden name would hopefully be a clue that it was her if he had not completely forgotten about her. She went back and forth about her profile picture, finally deciding on one from when she was four—the last time he would have set eyes on her. With a deep breath, she pulled up his page. She clicked on the message button and began typing. After five minutes and multiple do-overs, she was satisfied with her message and hit send.

Are you the same Neil Vincent who married Lillian Smythe and had a daughter?

June leaned back in her chair and looked at the letters glowing happily on her screen. She broke into a cold sweat as she waited for the tiny version of his profile pic to pop up. The seconds turned into minutes as she hovered her cursor over the button to recall the message. She stared intently at the screen, impatiently waiting for either the read indication or the bouncing dots to appear. She checked the time, seeing five minutes had passed.

"Three more minutes, then I'm recalling it." June leaned back in her chair, willing the response to come one moment and hoping she could chicken out and recall it the next.

After eight minutes had passed and she had just reached for the mouse to recall the message, his small profile pic appeared. Then the three bouncing dots. The dots disappeared. Then returned. Then disappeared again. She waited for them to come back once more, but they did not.

She stood and went to the restroom, taking her phone with her so she could read any response as soon as he sent it. As she washed her hands, she felt the crushing weight of disappointment. Deciding to just get ready for bed, she brushed her teeth and washed her face. It was when she was sliding under the covers that she let herself look at her phone one last time.

"Son of a—" she muttered as she saw she had missed a message from her biological father.

`Is this June-Bug?`

She frowned.

`Yes. But can you not call me that? Please?`

Okay. June. How are you?

Good.

She watched as the dots bounced for an eternity.

I don't really know what to say, other than I'm really happy to hear from you. I think about you often and wonder what you're up to.

This brought a smile to her face.

You do?

I do. How are you overall? Are you happy? Healthy? Are you married? Am I a grandfather?

June took in the rapid-fire questions. She was wondering how to answer them when another message popped up.

Sorry. Probably too much to ask too soon.

No. You're good. I'm happy overall. I guess I'm healthy. I'm recently divorced actually. And I have a four-year-old son.

When the bouncing dots did not appear, June sat up in bed, unsure if this was a good or bad sign. Her anxiety spiked as she questioned the wisdom of her actions. Then the dots began to dance.

```
Wow! I can't believe it. I'm stunned.
So many questions. Do you have any for
me as I process this?
```

June paused for a moment, unprepared for his enthusiastic but gentle responses.

```
Are you happy? Remarried? Do I have a
brother and/or sister?
```

```
Overall, I'm happy, but there's a
you-sized hole in my heart. I am remar-
ried. And you have two sisters.
```

```
I can't wait to meet them.
```

Once more the dots did not immediately start dancing. After a few moments, she again felt the anxiety swell. The moments turned into minutes. She felt the urge to throw her phone across the room. She reviewed the conversation, realizing that maybe she pushed too far too soon. An insistent bladder gave her the excuse to get a short distance away, and this time she left her phone.

When she returned, the dots were bouncing, and she held her breath for Neil's response. June had to exhale when nothing came. The dots just kept bouncing, almost as if the other end kept typing, erasing, and typing again. Just as she was about to say she was sorry, a message popped up on the screen.

```
Sorry, June. This is uncharted ter-
ritory for me, and I don't know what the
right thing to say is. I mean, as for
meeting your sisters, I'd need to talk
it over with my wife. I want you as part
of my life. I always have. And as much
as I've dreamed about this day and want
to see you as soon as possible, a lot has
changed. I want to do this right. Would
you be open to meeting with a thera-
pist? Perhaps we could do Zoom sessions
at first?
```

June didn't give herself time to think too far ahead, jumping at this chance.

```
It'll take some doing, but I think I
can do that.
```

```
Great! I'll do some research. Perhaps
your mother knows a good therapist?
```

It was June's turn to hesitate.

That may not be a good idea.

Your mother doesn't know you're reaching out to me, does she?

No. Does that change things?

I dunno. Maybe? But my gut tells me it doesn't. You're an adult. You can do what you want. I'm not going to push you to tell her. I know how Lillian can be. I'll work on finding a therapist on my end—not to pressure you, but I just want to be ready if you decide you're up for it.

Thank you … Dad? Neil? What do I call you?

Once more there was a pause on the distant end.

Please don't think I'm a jerk if I tell you "Dad" stings a little. Probably the same way June-Bug stung you. Would just Neil work? Until me calling you that other name doesn't sting anymore?

His optimism was contagious.

That would be fair.

Good. Are you good?

I am. Thank you, Neil.

I'll let you know when I've found someone to help us through this, but I'll leave the ball in your court as to how much or how little you want to chat until then.

Thank you.

One other thing. You don't need to say it to me. Just know I love you.

The last three words hit June like a ton of bricks. It felt good that he said it, but she could not bring herself to say it to him. Not yet.

Can I just say good night and have you not be offended?

Of course. Good night, June.

She put her phone face down beside her before crying herself to sleep, her tears a confused mixture of joy and pain.

XIX

June parked her Charger where Emily had when she'd brought her to Sara-Lyn's house. A raven cawed as she knocked on the door. When she turned, the obsidian bird glided down from a tree and landed on her car. Its head twitched as it studied her, its gaze hypnotizing.

"What are you looking at?" Sara-Lyn's voice jolted her from the raven's trance.

"Just a raven. He flew down from the trees and landed on my car."

"Interesting." Sara-Lyn leaned out her door to look at the bird. "Some believe that when a raven visits out of the blue, it means that things are changing and that you are about to see your true self."

"I feel like I should know who I am already," June answered, her voice heavy.

Sara-Lyn laid a hand on June's shoulder and smiled warmly. "Some people live their entire life never meeting their authentic self." She stared at June intently. "Is everything all right? You look tired."

June yawned as if on cue. "I haven't gotten much sleep recently. I had to take Mikey to the ER this week. He claimed something attacked him. He had marks on his neck that looked like someone tried to choke him. The doctor questioned us like he suspected abuse." She shook her head in defeat.

"Come, we have a Tarot lesson planned. And this sounds like the perfect time for a reading."

"What is Tarot?" June asked as she settled down at her host's kitchen table after following her inside. "Is it demonic?"

Sara-Lyn chuckled. "No, that's just propaganda. Tarot is occult and mystical, but it comes from what was essentially a parlor game in the 1400s." She produced a deck and handed it to June. "First, we need to know a question you want to ask the cards."

"Will I be rich?" June said with a smirk.

Sara-Lyn shook her head. "I know you're joking, but that's not the way it works. Tarot works best for giving insight into general forces shaping your life. What's something that you feel you need guidance on, not direction?"

June considered her words. "How can I move past the rut I'm in?"

"That's better," Sara-Lyn said and indicated the cards June had idly been turning over in her hands. "Shuffle."

"Any particular way?"

"... If you think it's good enough, it's good enough."

"Just however you shuffle any deck of cards."

June shuffled the deck Sara-Lyn gave her, an awkward cutting of cards and mushing them together. "Is that good enough?"

"I'm just here to read the cards, not give you step-by-step instructions. A lot of a successful reading depends on intuition. If you think it's good enough, it's good enough."

June handed the deck back to Sara-Lyn.

"Now pick a card."

"From the top?"

"From the top. The bottom. Third one from the center toward the top. Whatever cards call to you. Pick five and lay them down as you pull them."

June began pulling and placing them on the table between her and Sara-Lyn. She hesitated as she started to pull the fourth card.

"What's wrong?"

"I was just thinking Mom would be so mad if she knew I was here."

"What about Michael?"

"He'd be mad, too," June said as she pulled the card the rest of the way out and laid it down, "but Mom would also be disappointed." She pulled her final card.

Sara-Lyn nodded before beginning. "Okay, this first card is telling us what's happening now." She indicated that June should flip the card, and she took a deep breath when it revealed the image of a stained glass window. In it, a heart pierced by three swords hung above a cloud populated by flying doves, and the image was upside down. Sara-Lyn placed her hand on

June's. "The Three of Swords. Let's take a deep breath together." She took another deep breath and indicated June should do the same.

"That bad?"

"With this card, it's good to take a moment and just breathe, especially when it's inverted. It means great change is coming from a great loss. Now, know that this loss could be behind you. The divorce, Charlie Peterson dying, or both."

"Isn't loss like celebratory deaths? It comes in threes?" June asked.

"Do you think it could be something else? Are you feeling you could lose something or someone else?"

"Maybe. My divorce and Grandpa Charlie's death don't feel right."

"Interesting. Let's move on to the next card, which represents how you'll deal with what's going on."

June turned the card over revealing a peasant holding a staff and defending himself against six floating staffs on the edge of a precipice.

"The Seven of Wands. This card is about you rising to the top. See him standing on the hill?"

June studied the card. "Yes, so this is a good card?" She smiled.

Sara-Lyn looked down. "It means your rise to the top is not going to be easy. See how he's fighting the other wands? Someone is throwing up roadblocks and may have an active interest in holding you back. Any idea who?"

June thought for a moment. "My mother or maybe my father."

"Why do you think Lillian and Michael want to throw obstacles in your path?"

June shook her head. "Lillian, yes, but Michael, no. I'm talking about my biological father. I want to know him, but Mom doesn't want me to have anything to do with him. She's done everything she can to stop me."

"Has she?"

June looked away with the shame of a child who had done something her parents did not want her to do. "No. Emily helped me track him down. I reached out to him on Facebook."

"That's good. The point of this card is that while the path is difficult, it can be overcome." She motioned for June to turn over the next card, a noble looking over a low wall. In each hand was a staff like in the last card. "Two of Wands. An explorer hesitates as he looks out over the horizon trying to figure out what to do next."

"So, I'm indecisive?"

"Are you?" Sara-Lyn cocked an eyebrow. "Hesitation is not always bad. It means a person is looking before she leaps. In this case, I feel like it's a good thing. The first two cards indicate you're in a perilous place and you have to be careful. If you're cautious, you'll come out the other side of this moment a changed person and one who's probably going to be the better for it. Now, about the next card, I'm really interested in seeing what that is."

"Why?" June asked.

"It's the card that tells us something is leaving, and your thoughts lurched to your mother as you pulled it."

June's heart skipped a beat. "I'm going to lose my mother?" She had to fight back tears. "Maybe I should just tell my biological father I don't want to talk to him anymore."

Sara-Lyn put a hand on June's. "No, that's not what I meant. This card could mean any number of things. Yes, someone could exit your life, but it could also be that you could find love or closure or even success and wealth."

"Then what does me thinking about Mom have to do with anything?"

"It may not be your card. Let's find out."

The upside-down imagery of Adam and Eve standing in the Garden of Eden surprised June. Behind them was the tree of knowledge, complete with a serpent and the burning bush. Above them was God or at least an angel.

"I didn't think it'd have such Christian symbolism, being occult and all."

"There are many types of decks and not all of them are Western in nature. Since I grew up in this culture, I use decks with art that makes sense to me culturally. In terms of spirituality, it's going to be heavily Christian." She studied the card. "The Lovers, inverted."

"Upside down, so love turned on its head. Does that mean my divorce?"

Sara-Lyn's face screwed into a look of confusion. "Maybe. We're talking about what's leaving so it kind of makes sense, but does it feel right to you?"

"It sounds good, but it doesn't feel right as I speak it. What else could it mean?"

"Several things. When it's inverted, it means a love that's soured somehow. Not necessarily romantic love. It could be the loss of a job someone loves, then a sour career. What's left when love sours?"

"Hate?" June offered.

Sara-Lyn shook her head. "That's the case way too often. But remember, this may not be your card. You were thinking about Lillian, and she looms heavily over you. I recommend that you pay attention to it, but keep in mind that it may have been laid in error."

"So, think before I leap?" June asked.

"Yes." Sara-Lyn smiled happily.

"Let's see my last card." June flipped it over.

"Nine of Swords. The swords love you today." The card displayed a blond girl sitting up in bed, nine swords pointing at her. "I know you don't sleep well. This suits you."

June slumped in her chair. "So, I'm going to be an insomniac for the rest of my life?"

Sara-Lyn shook her head and picked up the card. "Not necessarily. Something is keeping you awake because you're aware of it. The nines in general means maturing, which makes sense because the fifth card means what is arriving. If this were the first card, I'd say we need to focus on your insomnia. However, in this position, I think we're talking about metaphorically waking up to the realities around you. Things are changing for you, June. It looks like a difficult path, but it's not without hope."

XX

Lillian watched as June left her room, trying to disguise a frown. "Looking good. I didn't realize this was a date."

June was wearing a breezy maxi dress that showed just a hint of cleavage. Lillian had never fully approved of Emily's bisexuality, and she wondered if the divorce had radically altered who June was.

"Mom!" June exclaimed. "We're just friends!"

Lillian's expression betrayed that she wasn't convinced. She placed a gentle hand on June's arm. "It makes sense, but please be discreet. Michael will screw himself into the roof."

"Mom! I just want to go out looking pretty. It doesn't have to be sexual."

Lillian's smile returned. "Okay. If you say so. Just remember you can always talk to me. I love our tea-time chats."

June's expression softened. "Me too, but there's nothing to say."

Lillian leaned close—conspiratorially close. "Honestly, you can do better."

"Mom! Enough!" June huffed. "I think she's here."

Lillian watched as June disappeared downstairs. Taking a deep breath, she fought the urge to immediately bolt into June's room. Something was off about her daughter, and she wanted to get to the bottom of it. When she had approached Michael about helping her hack June's password, he refused. One of the things he always stood his ground on was snooping in their daughter's private life. She was on her own, and the best hope she had was when she was alone in the house. Michael and Mikey were at the movies, so as soon as she heard the door open and close behind June, she hurried to her room.

She went straight for the laptop. Her heart sank a little at the blank screen. She slid her finger along the mousepad, hoping that it was just asleep and not locked. The screen woke up and a picture of June and Mikey stared back at her, along with June's desktop instead of a lock screen. If she were Michael, she would have thanked God. She opened Chrome.

"Please stay logged in," she said as she opened TikTok, then Instagram, and then Twitter. There was nothing of interest in her posts or messages. Finally, she tried Facebook. She took a seat and began scrolling through June's posts and looking at her Messenger.

Lillian's chest heaved as she took a deep, cleansing breath and then let it out. June's social media life was filled with memes, Mikey, and school—incredibly banal. She did pay close attention to the last messages between June and Emily. She was convinced they were flirting. Regardless, she leaned back in June's chair, relieved, and considered locking the computer and going about her night. That's when she noticed Edge was running. She clicked on the icon, and it opened straight to Facebook. Her heart stopped when she saw the Messenger notification. June had a new message—from Neil.

For a few moments, she sat quivering in rage. She fought the urge to respond to the latest message. She knew she had to be smart about how she handled this situation. All she could see were the last few messages, the most recent being from Neil:

```
Hey, June-Bug. I've talked to that
psychologist, and she's willing to do
talk therapy over Zoom. I know it may be
awkward, but it's for the best that we
have help as we reconnect. She did say
that maybe a quick informal Zoom might
be good to break the ice. She doesn't
need to be there for that but said may-
be limit it to 5-10 minutes and keep
it light.
```

> Oops! Sorry for calling you "J-B."
> I'm just letting myself feel a little
> excited right now!

Something had to be done. How many lies had her ex-husband already told her daughter about his "side" of their relationship? She knew that even if they hadn't discussed his bullshit sob story yet, they would eventually. She dug her fingernails into her palms at the thought. The pain centered her enough that she locked the laptop and headed to the basement to fully get a grip. She stopped by her office to get the piece of taillight she took from Charlie's house.

Rubbing the rough edges of the red shard calmed her as her feet touched the cool basement floor. She stopped to remove her socks, the cold on her feet a good counter to the burning rage in her chest. Drawn like a magnet, she hurried to the far corner of the basement. There, she did something she only did in absolute privacy. Lillian screamed a loud, piercing wail of hatred for her ex-husband. In her bleakest moments, the darkness would whisper back. As her throat began to scratch and her voice gave out, she felt grounded. Lillian closed her eyes and waited. She heard the whisper.

Neil must die.

§

Outside, on the edge of the wood by The Circle, the albino stag lowered its head. It did not look up at the sound of a raven taking wing from its perch above him.

XXI

Dinner had been fantastic. Mike's Steakhouse sat 30 minutes north of Junction Falls, and June passed it every day on her way to college. It was her favorite steak place, but, as the local four-star restaurant, she only dined there when Lillian and Michael were buying. Every time she drove by, she promised herself that someday she would be able to take herself there.

Until then, she was thankful that Emily's editor had given her an under-the-table bonus of gift certificates to Mike's. Her friend asked her to go spend them with her, and June happily agreed. She even played along with Em's half-jokes about it being a date. She relaxed in the wooden chair, sipping a third glass of wine as her meal settled.

Her friend's voice brought her back to the present. "Earth to June," Emily teased.

She turned to her friend and offered a coy smile as she looked at the last few red swallows of Pinot Noir.

"Well, why don't you tell me what's been bothering you all night?"

Emily swirled the remainder of her Sprite and whiskey. "It's better discussed on the way home. It's a little too public here. Besides, it's been nice just chatting about nothing heavy."

June's expression warmed. "Especially considering the recent incident with Mikey." She paused. "Is that bad—a mother not wanting to talk about her kids every chance she gets?"

Emily considered it for a moment. "I can't say. I mean, I don't think so. But then again, I'm pretty 'meh' on all things kids. Is *that* bad?"

June weighed her friend's words. "I don't think so. Not everyone is cut out to be a parent. But at the same time, Mikey is pretty great."

"Exactly. I can live vicariously through the clones you and Gerica make."

"Have you ever wanted kids? Like growing up?"

"When I was really young. I mean, sometimes I do think about it. If the right person were to come along and put a ring on it, sure." She considered the last of her drink. "Honestly, when I was really little, I was all about taking care of baby dolls, but when my little brother was born …" Emily tapered off with a grimace.

"David was a home birth, right?"

Emily nodded. "Yep." She emphasized the "p" and stared right through June. "The way Mom was crying and screaming. And you know me, Lil' Miss Curiosity. I didn't listen, and, when Dad was distracted, I sneaked into the bedroom and saw him crown." She shuddered at the memory. "Ever since then, I've never wanted children outside of some fleeting moments. I just don't want to pay the physical price."

June looked down at her empty wine glass, hiding a smile. "I'm sorry to trigger old trauma."

"It's okay. I'm tough," Emily joked. "Now, what do you say we get out of here?"

June slipped her arm around Emily's and laid her head on the other girl's shoulder as they strolled into the night. "Thank you for a wonderful evening."

"Don't worry about it."

When they got to the car, Emily turned to June. "Can I just say that your eyes are an amazing green?"

"Even though they're Neil's?" The words spilled out, adding an awkward pause to the compliment.

"I don't know him. And if I did? It wouldn't matter because I don't see his eyes. I see yours."

A smile lit up June's face in the darkening parking lot. Emily hugged her. Both women wiped away a tear.

June spoke. "Changing the subject, what's been bugging you all night?"

"I don't know, June." Emily looked around nervously.

"Now you've got me worried. You can't leave me hanging."

"Okay, but not here in the open. Let's just get on the road."

June slid into the passenger seat and buckled up as Emily stepped around the vehicle. "Why so serious?"

she asked as her friend slid into the driver's seat and started the car.

"Something's been bugging me ever since the night Charlie died."

"Well, it's a messed-up situation. Gerica lost her grandfather—"

"No, not that. I mean, yes, it is. But what about the other guy?" Emily said as she pulled out of the parking lot and made her way to the overpass about a half mile away.

"What about him? Mom said he was some meth head who succumbed to his wounds. He abused his body with drugs. He got what he deserved if you ask me."

"I can understand that, but listen. I've been assigned to write about Charlie's life. A human-interest piece that goes beyond the obituary. He only had a daughter, so he was the last to carry the Peterson name, which is big news in Junction Falls."

"Okay? What does this have to do with anything? So what?"

"I interviewed some of the staff working that night. They all say Bancroft was alert. Sure, he was in pain from the gunshot wound, but he's an addict. They didn't know for sure what was in his system, and they were under strict orders not to give him anything that could react with whatever drugs he might have taken earlier that night."

"Why are you telling me all this?" June asked in confusion.

Emily stared into the darkness surrounding her headlights. "I think someone killed him."

June let out an awkward laugh before looking out her window. "Good riddance?"

"June, seriously. Someone took his life. Without a trial. And that someone, I believe, took an oath to do no harm." Emily glanced at June.

June was watching her reflection as the realization dawned on her. "Emily, don't go there."

"Think about it. I may be wrong, but I don't think so," Emily pressed, pushing June into a figurative corner.

"Emily, my mom can be a hard ass and cold sometimes." June could not let the attack against her mom, for all Lillian's faults, stand. It was absurd. "But she's not going to kill someone like some avenging angel." She crossed her arms across her chest in an attempt to close the conversation.

"Someone gave him morphine," Emily said with an exasperated sigh, keeping her eyes on the road. "I did some digging, and it wasn't there when he was alive. No one else has the motive." She took a deep breath before delivering the next blow. "Isn't she Charlie's executor?"

"Shut up, Em! I don't want to hear it anymore!" June slammed her fist against the dashboard. "Just because you and Mom never got along doesn't make her some cold-hearted bitch capable of murder!" She twisted in her seat to face Emily, her voice just short of a yell. "Fuck! You two are so alike. No wonder you never got along!" June held back tears.

The remainder of the drive featured only the sound of the radio playing.

§

Lillian sat at the kitchen table drinking a cup of tea while Mikey slept and Michael tended to some church business. The storm of her rage had passed, leaving her calm. She had her next target and needed to consider how she would deliver justice once more. June's slamming the door when she entered the house did not even startle her.

"Have a good evening, dear?" She sipped her tea.

"Everything is fine," June growled as she slipped off her sandals. "Is Mikey asleep?"

"Yes, Michael put him down about a half hour ago. Can I make you a cup of tea?"

"That sounds great. I'll be back."

"Take your time, dear," Lillian said with a serene smile.

XXII

"Hi, Daddy!" June said, putting her backpack on a kitchen chair before kissing him on the cheek.

"You're happy?" Michael asked with a tone of surprise in his voice. "Good day at school?"

"Very! Got an A on my test in that Political Economy class!"

"That was one of the courses you were sweating, wasn't it?"

June nodded as she poured herself a celebratory Coke. "Yep. Still, I'll be glad when it's all over and I'm done and graduated." She emphasized each syllable in the word and hopped up on the counter just like she did growing up. "How's Mikey?"

"Mommy!" On cue, her child burst into the room, bumping the chair her backpack sat on and sending the contents spewing forth across the floor.

June's eyes went wide in horror as all 78 cards from the Tarot deck Sara-Lyn gave her splayed across the floor. Her eyes focused on one in particular: The Ace of Swords. Her mind vaguely remembered reading that it was a disruptive card that meant sweeping change and the search for truth. She also remembered that swords could cut both ways, so their appearance could be a good or ill omen.

"What. Is. This?" Michael's tone was cold and full of restrained anger.

Mikey burst into tears, diverting June from picking up the spilled deck.

"Devil cards? In my house?" He bent over and picked two up and showed them to June. "Death? The Hanged Man? What does this mean? I'm going to die? Be killed? Just for touching the cursed things? Or what about Mikey? He's the one who knocked them over!"

"Daddy, I don't know! I've only been reading—"

"Mommy! I don't wanna die!" Mikey screeched.

"Look what you did!" June yelled at her father.

"Don't change the subject!" he shouted back. "How long have you been 'reading'?" His tone switched from angry to mocking.

"Just a few weeks." She clutched Mikey to her chest and watched as Michael gathered the cards.

"Who gave them to you? That's the rule, right? Someone has to give them to you?"

"N-no one," June stuttered.

"Don't lie to me, June. This may not be a church, but it's still a house of God you're defiling!" His eyes went wide. "Was it the witch? I knew you were spending more time with that friend of yours, and her family is trouble! That damned Witch of Endor! Even when she was dating Uncle Steve, your grandparents thought she was trouble."

"You don't know that!"

Michael spun on her. "Oh? Why so defensive? Tell me it wasn't her! Go ahead and lie to a minister of the Word!"

June looked away.

"I knew it! You are not to see that woman ever again! Understand?" His tone abruptly softened as a tear slid down June's cheek. "June, it's just that we're talking about your eternal soul. Do not give yourself to Satan like this."

"What are you going to do with them?" She sniffled.

"Cast them where they belong," he said, picking up the last few before standing and making his way outside, grabbing the lighter.

"No!" June cried.

Michael spun on her. "Take my grandson upstairs, and go to your room!"

June obeyed as she felt herself regress to childhood once again, a dark inversion of her previous joy.

"What happened?" Mikey asked as she carried him upstairs.

"Nothing, baby. Mommy did something to make Paw-Paw angry. It'll be okay."

"Mommy did something bad?"

"Depends on who you ask," she said as he stuck his thumb in his mouth.

After setting him on his bed, she watched Michael burn her Tarot deck through the window.

XXIII

Lillian had barely gotten in the door when Michael greeted her with a growl instead of a kiss.

"We need to talk," he said as he turned and walked toward her office, taking a seat behind her desk.

She slid into one of the chairs facing him. These were somehow even less comfortable than her regular chair.

"What's up?" She kept her tone light, even though she disapproved of him taking her seat—a power move he reserved for times he intended to stand his ground against her. She had a power move of her own, but it had to be made at just the right time.

"It's June. She's dabbling in Satanism."

Lillian had braced for almost anything but that. While she knew June had an irrational interest in the paranormal, she did not think it crossed the line into Devil worship.

"What makes you say that?"

"She's been carrying a Tarot deck around with her."

Lillian cocked her head. "Openly?"

"No, in her backpack," Michael said, his eyes filled with anger.

"You were going through her backpack?" She tried to keep any hint of accusation out of her voice. She tried.

"Seriously, Lillian? You're the one with a history of snooping. You always take her side against me. Is it because I'm just the adoptive father? Or is it because I'm a man?" He held up his hand when she started to reply. "You know what? I don't care. It doesn't matter. Mikey knocked her backpack over, and her deck spilled out all over the floor. Most of the cards fell face down, but the two that were facing up were 'Death' and some 'Hanged Man.' What kind of evil is she bringing in that we don't know about? Should we check her room for a Ouija board?"

"I just wanted to know if you were going through her stuff because she's in a delicate place right now. I don't think it's a good idea that you go poking around in her things like when she was a teenager." Lillian attempted to swing the conversation from the spiritual to the psychological.

Michael replied with a derisive snort. "Typical. Taking her side against all others—including me. How many times have I hung with you to present a unified front when it was something that mattered to you? But when it comes to something someone else sees an issue with, it's mother and daughter against the world! To Hell with everybody else!"

Lillian did her best to quell the rage building up inside her. "It's different!" she snapped back. "You develop habits when you've been a single mother of a sick kid!" she could not help but hiss. "And they die hard, even when you remarry a terrific man."

"Yes, darling, I know, you're the 'Mother of the Year,'" Michael said, causing her to sit up straight. Michael held up his hand. "That came out wrong. That award was well deserved. It's just that you don't have to go it alone anymore, and you haven't for some time. Most of the time we make a pretty good team and you support me, but sometimes you *do* undermine me."

She looked away from him in feigned shame. Now was the time for her power move. "I'm sorry. You're right." She sniffled a little.

He sighed. "I'm just worried. I don't want to lose her or our grandson to Lucifer." He stood and came around from the other side of the desk and leaned against it. "I don't know if Tarot is the extent of it or if she's involved with practicing actual magic. What do you think we should do?"

Lillian looked up at him. "Right now? I don't know. Perhaps we should just sleep on it." She began unbuttoning the top of her blouse. "Talk to June in the morning as a team? After we've had a chance to destress?" She smiled.

He tried to look away and stay focused, but his eyes continued to be drawn to his wife's cleavage. "That's not fair." His tone was as dejected as it was anxious.

"No, I guess it's not." She pulled her blouse open a little more.

"How many arguments have you won this way?" he said as he pulled her out of the chair and into his arms.

"All of them?" She smiled in victory.

He did not argue. He just lifted her off her feet and carried her to bed.

XXIV

The Kentucky countryside sped past Lillian's car as she made a detour on the way to the annual meeting of the National Organization of State Offices of Rural Health in Cincinnati. Since COVID-19, she preferred to drive. Being enclosed in a pressurized metal tube and imagining respiratory viruses floating in the cabin was not her idea of fun. It also had the benefit of making her three-hour detour possible. Her rage seethed as she made the trip. Her trap was set this morning when she messaged Neil from a new Facebook account. As the miles ticked by, she replayed the messages in her head.

Hi, Dad. I went ahead and told Mom about us talking. She went through the roof! I showed her the account but not our messages. She was SO pissed that I created a new account, so please respond to this one since my other is now compromised. She can be such an unreasonable bitch!

The stupid bastard fell for her catfishing attempt.

I guess calling me "Dad" is fair for my slip-up. :) Okay, I'll ignore messages from the other account. But hey, don't be too hard on your mom. Divorces are tough, and people make mistakes. It gets hard to see through all the pain and understand another's point of view.

The last message gave her pause. Not knowing how to respond, she didn't. She even considered coming clean to June about him for half a second. Then another message popped up.

It doesn't help that to me she was an actual bitch!

This made Lillian's blood boil, leaving no room for more than that half-second of doubt.

That she can be! Anyway, Mom is away for work, and I'm going to have the house all to myself from about 2 to 6. Does that work for that quick Zoom call?

Lillian had ground her teeth while typing.

184

Sure! I can take off a little early. 4 sound good? The wife is taking our
kids to see her parents tonight. I'll be
alone, too. I'll set up the Zoom. What's
your email?

Lillian gave him a fake email she had just created. She wondered if she should better cover her tracks, but a 47-year-old man having a heart attack while home alone would not raise any serious red flags.

4 sounds good!

This was all June's fault. Had she just given Lillian more time to come to terms with her wanting to know more, things would've been fine. In another six months or a year, she would have told June everything about the sperm donor. Well, almost everything. But June had crossed a line. Lillian could not help but consider his intrusion a threat. Now that she had taken a life to deliver justice, taking a life in self-defense would be easy.

She was scheduled to present in two days, and she did not care if she missed check-in and discussion panels. She had occasionally cyber-stalked Neil before and knew he had moved on, remarried, and had children with the other woman. She hoped, for the wife and kids' sakes, that Neil had grown up and did not torture them as he did her.

Her heart rate quickened as she slowed and passed his house. There wasn't a car parked in front. She parked on another street and got out. She wore running pants and a plain gray t-shirt. Her hair was pulled into a ponytail with sunglasses covering her eyes. She blended in as she started to walk through the neighborhood. In one hand, she carried a water bottle, tightly sealed.

The clear liquid sloshing around the bottom was not water. Dimethyl sulfide, or DMSO, was a compound that was readily absorbed by the skin and could carry other compounds into a person's system. It was used to carry medicines and pain relievers into the bloodstream. However, it, like the medicines it introduced, could be misused.

Like many other hospitals, Lillian's had begun dispensing a new drug that provided cancer patients with long-term pain relief. This new treatment involved injecting a minuscule amount of tetrodotoxin, which was found in blowfish. In tiny amounts, it eased the suffering of cancer patients. In the amount that nature had armed the blowfish with, the substance, more toxic than cyanide, could produce a quick death—a death that would present as a heart attack unless the coroner specifically tested for the poison.

As she approached the house on foot, she scanned the quiet neighborhood. Hyperalert, she did not see movement in any window she passed. If anyone was home, they were otherwise occupied. Doing this in daylight and with the chemicals involved was a bold plan. Lillian worried that he might have had a camera doorbell or other security camera, but she relaxed and exhaled slowly when she didn't see one.

Pausing at the end of the driveway, she quickly put on clear latex gloves and pulled gauze from her pocket. She opened the storm door and made a show of knocking. She unscrewed the cap and swiftly wet the gauze, careful to not splatter the lethal liquid. She wiped the doorknob until it glistened with a wet sheen. She then shoved the gauze into the poison bottle. Without a second thought, she turned and left.

Under the shadowy cover of trees, she expertly removed her gloves inside out so the side slick with toxin would be contained. She balled it in her gloved hand and repeated the process. She breathed deeply before dropping them and the bottle into the grass. Had she made a mistake, she would have been dead in 15 seconds. She pulled from her bra a folded gallon-sized Ziploc bag. She turned it inside out and retrieved the water bottle and gloves as if picking up after a dog. A minute later, with the bag sealed and its contents concealed by a plastic shopping bag, she made her way back to her car. She wanted to grab a quick bite before her ex got home.

§

Gary Numan's "Cars" was playing as Neil Vincent put his car in park. A sense of joy had buoyed him throughout the day. He was going to see and hear his daughter for the first time in almost 20 years. He had shared the message with a co-worker, and she gave him a happy hug. He had to pretend his eyes were not welling with tears, telling his colleagues it must be allergies.

Running his fingers through long, wavy salt-and-pepper hair, he looked at the house's darkened windows. He felt the absence of his wife and two children, but he knew he had to handle this situation on his own and delicately. Still, if June decided to show him his grandson, he had the go-ahead from his wife to put June's sisters on camera when he felt the time was right. The girls were anxious to meet their mysterious older sister.

He pulled a worn and tattered picture of June from the inside pocket of his sport coat. He had carried it to Hell and back again for almost two decades. In another time and place, with the stroke of his pen, she became another man's daughter. He told himself severing this piece of his soul was the right thing to do. Most days, despite his gut's lingering doubts, he even believed it. But now, regardless, father and daughter would be reunited.

Neil replaced the picture in his pocket before opening the car door and setting his prosthetic foot on the driveway. He paused. His gut was telling him to stay in the car or perhaps go see a movie. It screamed at him to do anything but enter the empty house. He closed his eyes and counted to 10, calming himself. His gut had saved his life in Kuwait. Had he not followed its lead, the improvised explosive device would have taken more than half of his leg. This was different. This was just nerves about putting the right foot forward with his estranged child.

He opened his eyes. His gut had grown too sensitive since then, too cautious. Besides, he convinced himself that he was home and he was safe. Suppressing his hunch, he got out of his car and stepped to his front door.

He slid his key into the deadbolt and turned. He thought it was odd that he heard his dogs outside. He could remember bringing them in that morning, but he also found himself increasingly misremembering things as he aged. He grabbed the door handle and pushed the latch to open the door. He took two steps inside and dropped his briefcase as an intense pain gripped his chest. He fell to his knees before toppling forward.

Fuck! I'm having a heart attack!

He heard soft footfalls behind him. Something was oddly familiar about them. His mind, fighting for survival, dug up deeply buried memories. Familiar footfalls. Intense pain. It was as if he'd said her name aloud.

When he and Lillian were getting engaged, she had told him that, during her internship, she learned how to kill a person and make it look natural. Back then, he had found her excitement at this knowledge oddly endearing. She mentioned some solvent mixed with poison from some fish the Chinese ate. She joked that if her husband ever cheated on her, this is how she would kill him—her grin the same one he would later recognize meant she was only half-joking

He managed to roll over and look up, meeting the cold eyes of his ex-wife.

"F-fish poison," he uttered—his final words.

As Neil shed his mortal coil, he saw Lillian disappear into the guest bedroom. With new sight, he caught a glimpse of her soul. It was cold, and it was evil. At that moment, he was made privy to all that she had done. He felt anger and an overpowering desire to protect his daughter and grandson. He was in turmoil as his consciousness faded to black.

§

Lillian hummed. It was perfect—a symbol of all that was wrong with their marriage and how that chapter of her life was now definitively over. She was amazed he still had it. The damn bear had been a gift his parents had tried to give June when they were going through the divorce. She hated them, too. They always made excuses for their son's failures. This was so much better than the shard of taillight. No one would miss this, being too busy mourning the loss of a husband and father. She could send it to Mikey as a gift!

She could keep it in plain sight.

XXV

The tone of a text notification distracted June from her studies. She groaned seeing it was from Emily. She hadn't responded to her texts in the weeks since their argument. She appreciated the space her friend had given her to calm down and was slowly starting to think about talking to her again. She opened the message.

    June, I'm 5 minutes out. NEED TO TALK
    TO YOU!! Please!

She took a deep breath and considered the situation. It had to be something Emily considered important enough to wait to text her until she was so close that June had little opportunity to back out. She typed a two-letter response and hit send before she could change her mind.

A few moments went by, and she heard Emily's car pulling up to the house followed by the slamming of the car door. When she opened the door, she saw Emily running toward her, tears running down her cheeks.

"Emily! Oh my God! What happened?"

Emily just shook her head and wrapped June in a giant bear hug. "I'm so sorry." Her voice was soft and soothing. "I know you're still mad at me, but I couldn't just message you. I had to tell you in person. I'm so sorry, June."

"Emily," June's voice quivered with fear, "what's wrong?"

"It's your father. He-he's—" she faltered.

"Emily, what happened to Michael?" June pushed away from her friend to look her in the eye.

"Not your stepdad!" Emily almost shouted.

"What?" June felt her heart stop. "Neil?"

"I had alerts set to his name so if something came up I'd get an email." Emily struggled to catch her breath between sobs. "The obituary was posted in the *Edmonton Herald-News*. He had a heart attack. His wife found him, but it was too late. He was dead on arrival at the hospital." Emily choked out the bad news and hugged June again as she stood there dazed. "I'm here for you. Whatever you need. If you're still mad at me, I'll go."

Touched by her friend's loyalty and sensitivity even amid confused tears, June reached up and returned the embrace. She buried her face in Emily's shoulder and began to sob.

"It's not fair! I just started talking to him!" Her voice was muffled.

Emily guided her inside and to the living room sofa. June held her friend close. They had just been through this with Gerica, who would spend long minutes just sobbing over her loss.

June began to mumble from time to time. "We were going to reconnect … Why? … Why now?" It felt like hours had passed when June pulled away, wiping tears from her eyes and trying to compose herself. "Thanks, I needed that."

"Of course, June. Is Michael home?"

"No. It's just me and Mikey. I've got to get myself together before Dad gets home. He cannot know about any of this." She shook her head. "It fuckin' sucks. When I need a father and a pastor the most, I can't talk to him."

"Yeah, but if you told him, he'd probably take it better than Lillian."

"He would." June shook her head again. "But he'd still tell Mom, and that'd be problematic. That and he's still a little pissed at me."

"For what?"

"He found the Tarot deck Sara-Lyn gave me. Even burned them and accused me of falling into Satanism."

Emily scoffed. "This is why I'm agnostic. No dogma. Just 'I don't know.' Aunt Sara-Lyn helps people with loss, you know. Maybe you could run out to her place and see her?"

"But what about Mikey?"

193

"I've got Mikey. When's Michael coming home?"

"Late. Maybe nine."

"That gives you five hours to get there and get back." Emily's expression told June that this was not up for debate.

"Are you sure?" June asked, though Emily was already nodding. "Okay. If Michael gets home early or I get home late, tell him you stopped by to make up. We talked, we're on good terms, and you offered to watch Mikey as I went for a drive to clear my head from all the drama and studying."

"So, lie to your parents just like when we were in high school? Got it!" Emily smiled as the two friends hugged. "I'll call ahead and let Sara-Lyn know you're coming and what happened."

XXVI

June wiped her tears as she made her way to Sara-Lyn's door. She started to knock when the door flew open, and she was pulled into another embrace.

"I'm so sorry, dear. I know that doesn't help. Come inside. I just made some Earl Grey. I'll pour you a cup."

"Tea sounds wonderful," June said as she stepped inside.

"Do you take it with honey or sugar?"

"Honey sounds nice."

"I haven't heard from you in a while," Sara-Lyn stated as she poured the tea and mixed honey into both cups. "Everything okay?"

"No. Michael found my Tarot cards."

Sara-Lyn winced as if physically struck. "I bet that didn't go well. Did your Mom help you unscrew him from the ceiling or could you do that yourself?"

June chuckled a little—the first instance of levity she'd felt since Emily broke the news to her. "Mom

XAVIER POE KANE

helped." But that lightness faded as quickly as it came, immediately replaced by guilt for feeling anything but grief for the father she would never know.

"That's good. I take it they don't know you've been chat timing with Neil?"

June nodded, choosing not to correct "chat timing."

"Well, that's none of my business." Sara-Lyn handed June a cup of tea. "Let's have a seat on the couch and chat." She led June to a large sofa and love-seat from the early '80s.

While others may have scoffed at the dated maroon fabric, it was soft and comfortable, making June feel safe as she sunk into it. June sipped her tea. "I can't believe he's gone. We'd only had two chats over Messenger and now this."

"I know it may be of little comfort to you now, but just because the physical body ceases to function doesn't mean who he is ceases to be."

"I know I'll see him in Heaven, but I just wish I'd gotten some answers and actually heard his side of the story in person."

"Maybe you'll get that chance. Someone with your abilities should be able to speak to those who've moved on," Sara-Lyn said before taking a sip of her tea.

"You really think I have some ability?"

"I do. I just think so many spirits are trying to talk to you at once that you get overwhelmed and can't hear any of them."

"Can you teach me to do what you do?"

"I don't think your parents would approve."

June scoffed. "What do they know?" She shook her head. "Look at me. My life is a wreck. I'm back home as a single mother regressing to being 16 again. I'm finishing a degree I don't really care about."

"What is it you want?"

June sighed and leaned back into the plush love-seat. "I don't know. To be an adult and treated like one. Mom didn't want to relive her first marriage—that's fine and makes sense. But her selfishness cost me the chance of getting to know him and my siblings."

"You still have those opportunities. Perhaps his wife is open to getting to know you? She could tell you about him and some of his story. In time, you might meet his other children," Sara-Lyn said in a soothing tone.

"You mentioned talking to his spirit. Is that possible? How would that even work?"

"Unfortunately, it's not like picking up a phone and dialing a number. He needs to want to come through from the other side. It may take some time, too. Death is a change, and there's often a transition period to adjust. It's why we have ghosts; they're those who either don't know they've died, can't accept it, or just don't take it well."

"What do I need to do to listen to him?"

"It starts with a clear mind and meditation. When you're calm, at peace, and passive, you'll be able to hear them. Come. Let me show you how I meditate." Sara-Lyn stood and, dropping off empty teacups in the kitchen, headed to her basement. She pulled a stick of incense from a hexagonal package labeled "Serenity" and lit it.

"Wouldn't the 'Meditation' one be more appropriate?" June asked.

"That's just marketing. While some things may tend to produce better results for some people, meditation is a very personal and individualized experience. After I teach you the basics, you'll have to play around with it and find what's optimal for you." Sara-Lyn grabbed two crystals, one clear as glass and the other clear but a little cloudy. She eased her way to the floor. "It's not as easy as when I was your age," she said with a chuckle. "Enjoy this time in your life." She placed the crystals in front of her. "It's more precious than you know, and when you realize how precious, it'll be gone." She indicated June should sit across from her, the crystals between them.

June did as indicated. Her mentor pressed a polished turquoise stone into her hand.

"What's this for?"

"Just something to hold onto, a physical connection to aid in mindfulness. This next crystal is quartz. It's exceptionally clear and my favorite to focus on. The other is selenite, which helps communicate with angels. It's also very powerful with feminine energy and can help with healing."

"So should I—" June began to ask, but Sara-Lyn held up a hand.

"Remember, besides being calm and at peace, you need to be passive. Clear your mind of questions and let me guide you. Questioning an experience can be a way of resisting it. It can keep your mind distracted and closed instead of open."

June nodded, and Sara-Lyn's expression turned to that of a teacher with a prized student.

"Okay, focus on the clear," she instructed. "See how clear it is. Imagine your mind as clear from thought and question as that quartz is from contamination."

§

After 30 minutes, June began to tilt to one side. She threw an arm out to steady herself. "Damn it!" she spat, breaking Sara-Lyn's concentration.

"What's wrong?"

"Nothing. My mind has been clear, but nothing has come through." June pulled her legs to her chest and put her face between her knees. "Perhaps I don't have power."

"Oh, child," Sara-Lyn said lovingly. "It just takes time. Sometimes things buried in the subconscious get in the way. Anger. Doubt. Any strong emotion. Even joy. Is there anything bothering you?"

June sighed. "Yes. Lots of things. My biological father is dead. I have no answers. Michael is still upset with me. Plus, my relationship with Emily and some of the things she's said recently."

"Like what?"

"She thinks Mom killed the guy who broke into Grandpa Charlie's house."

Sara-Lyn recoiled in shock. "Really? Why?"

"Nothing more than coincidences. She doesn't have any evidence, and the two have never gotten along."

Sara-Lyn stared at June intently. "But you think there's something to it?"

"No!" June knee-jerked before taking a breath. "Well, I've been thinking about the Tarot reading and the card that could've been Mom's. It was about leaving and soured or lost love. Mom lost the last parental figure she had, so maybe she lost it and ..." her voice trailed as she stared at a point a thousand yards over Sara-Lyn's shoulder. "So, maybe?" she asked, coming back into the moment. "I don't know."

"This would be a powerful blockage. Part of being a medium is keeping oneself centered. Something like this is like a captured beast trapped deep underground, an animal clawing its way to the surface. Things trapped in our subconscious can block energy even when our mind is clear."

June looked away.

"You believe Emily, don't you?" Sara-Lyn put a hand on June's. "Or at least you're considering it?"

"Yes." The tears slid down June's cheek.

"There's something else itching at the back of your mind. A realization you're not wanting to think about."

June nodded. "What should I do?"

"Well, first step would be acknowledging what's gnawing at you—what you don't want to face."

"I have this insane idea that Mom was somehow involved in Neil's death," June blurted out before she could lose her courage.

Sara-Lyn didn't recoil this time. "You'd have to figure out if it's even possible first, then you can confront it." She placed a comforting hand on June's knee.

"What's the second step?"

"Letting Emily know you're not upset at her and letting the friendship heal. Then you need to decide for yourself what to believe."

§

Returning home, June found Emily on the couch reading a book.

"Emily, we need to talk. About your thoughts about Lillian."

She abruptly closed her book and sat up. "Nothing to talk about. It was my suspicious mind. I've been thinking about it, and I—" Emily paused, starting to get choked up. "I-I should've done my due diligence and only talked to you once I had something solid."

"No, Em. I mean, yes, evidence would be nice, but sometimes you have to go with your gut to save someone you care about." June shook her head. "Besides, you made solid points. I think I was so upset because I couldn't—" she faltered. "I couldn't disagree with you." She plopped on the couch with a sigh, trying to stop herself from crying again. "I can't help but wonder if she could be connected to Neil's death. Going through Beaumont would only add three hours of drive time to the fastest route between here and Cincinnati. I looked it up."

"Are you serious?"

June knew the look on Emily's face meant her mental gears were working it out.

"But how would she fake a heart attack?" Emily shook her head. "She's smart, but is she that smart?"

June just shrugged. "I don't know." She fell silent as her mind struggled to solve the assumed mystery of Neil's passing. "What am I going to do? What if she did? What does that mean?"

Emily plopped beside her. "You can't stay here. Come move in with me."

June laughed. "Despite your best efforts, my mom still doesn't like you. We had a very uncomfortable talk before you took me out to dinner."

This made Emily fidget. "What about Michael?"

"I don't know."

"You could still move in."

June shook her head. "Into your two-bedroom duplex? I don't think it'd be good to share a room with Mikey."

"But seriously, what if your mom is a serial killer? What's stopping her from harming you? Or Mikey?" Emily was suddenly frantic.

"Jesus, Emily!" June shouted and jumped to her feet. "A serial killer? She's a doctor! That guy killed someone she loved! And Neil—" June cut herself off. "I'm her daughter! Look at how proud she was of being

'Mother of the Year' when we were growing up! She's the 'World's Best Dr. Mom'! Mikey and I—we're safe."

"For the time being," Emily said quietly, but June was already walking away.

XXVII

June sat outside, enjoying the warm late summer day. She had a blanket laid out on the ground, and she was studying game theory as Mikey climbed on the playset. He was giggling and that made her happy.

Following the ER trip, he seemed troubled, sticking to her like glue and fearing every shadow. At night, he would not sleep unless all the lights were on. Outside was a different story. In the warmth of the sun, he became his happy-go-lucky self once more. And as for her, she did her best studying and thinking in The Circle.

"Look, Mommy! The deer!" he shouted with glee, causing her to look up from her book as the large albino stag emerged from the grove of trees about 20 yards from the playset. He ran toward the magnificent creature. The stag lowered his head and allowed Mikey to pet him.

Smiling, she rose to her feet and walked toward

them. The animal always filled her with a warm sense of peace.

"Hello, old friend," she said, enjoying the feel of grass under her bare feet with every step. As she drew near, he lifted his head, allowing her to scratch the spot between his antlers.

"No one believes me when I say you're real." She knew that, somehow, the animal could understand her. "You always seem to know when you're needed."

As magical as The Circle had always been, it was even better when the stag was around. She looked down at Mikey and basked in the happy moment.

The sound of a large vehicle pulling up to the house caused the stag to look up. Mother and son turned to see what he was looking at. A UPS delivery truck had pulled up to the house. As silly of a gesture as it was, June turned to say good-bye to the deer, but he had disappeared.

The deer always disappeared.

The delivery man was stepping out of the back of the truck with a box almost large enough to hold Mikey. "June Williams?"

"Yes." She took the package from him, its lightness surprising her.

"Sign please." He held out his ruggedized tablet.

She put the box down to sign. "It's from Grandma! Let's take it inside and open it!"

Mikey nodded eagerly. "Okay! Let's go!" He ran ahead, standing on his tiptoes to open the door.

They headed right into the kitchen. June pulled a knife from the butcher block to cut through the tape and open the box. In the background, the UPS truck's tires crunched on gravel.

"Who do you think this is for?" She reached in and pulled out a blue and white teddy bear. "Is it for Mommy?"

"No," he replied coyly.

"Is it for Paw-Paw?"

"No," he giggled, the same shy tone in his angelic voice.

"Is it for Grandma?"

"Mommy, it's me!" He grinned wide.

"Are you sure?" She wanted to draw out the game a little while longer.

"Yes!" he squealed, reaching for the toy.

She took a moment to look at the bear. It had a sad expression, out of step with the fun coloring. She wondered if maybe the factory had put sad eyes on the bear by mistake. She shrugged and handed the plush to Mikey, who immediately ran off to the living room.

He returned a few moments later dragging the bear behind him. "Mommy, he wants to watch Star Wars. He says it's his favoritest movie!"

She looked out the window and then at her son. June thought about encouraging him to go back outside. It was beautiful weather—not a cloud in the sky. She longed for the peace The Circle offered her. However, it was the first time he had wanted to watch his cartoons since they had found him unconscious.

"Okay, let me put it on."

He squealed in delight and ran off toward the TV.

She started streaming the cartoon. "I'm just going to go outside and get my books. I'll be right back, okay?

"Okay, Mommy."

He was staring at the TV, and she shrugged and headed outside to bring in her books, laptop, and blanket, leaving Mikey alone.

He was staring at the TV ...

§

As the door banged shut, the darkness appeared and crept toward the child. Its tendrils unfurled toward him as the adventures of animated star warriors entranced him. He shuddered a little as the light in the room faded like a thundercloud passing in front of the sun.

He laughed happily at the antics of the droid chopper, but a tentacle of ethereal shadow started sliding toward the bear resting at his owner's side. It recoiled suddenly.

"Bear says not to be scared of you," Mikey said, not even bothering to turn around.

XXVIII

In need of a mental health day, June was taking a break from studying. While Mikey played with some toys, his new teddy bear at his side, June watched some *Haunted Houses*. This episode saw the family investigating a house on the other side of the state in St. Louis. It was the house that inspired William Peter Blatty to write the novel *The Exorcist*. She jumped and let out a little yelp as her cell vibrated in her pocket. This caused Mikey to look at her.

"You okay, Mommy?"

She checked the phone. "It's just Grandma."

"Grandma!" He shot to his feet.

"Hold on, big guy." She snapped her fingers, which was their signal to calm down.

He fell silent and pouted.

"Hi, Mom," she said.

"Hi, sweet pea," Lillian greeted, her voice tired and stressed.

June could hear the noise of the conference-goers in the background. "Have you given your presentation yet?" She got up and left the room so it wouldn't be hard to hear with Mikey playing. She heard him giggling, thankful for the positive change.

"No, not yet. I was about to go into the conference hall. How is Mikey doing? I don't hear him wailing in the background. Is that—is he actually giggling?"

June chuckled softly. "Believe it or not, he is. Ever since he got the bear, he's been calm. Thank you. It's a real lifesaver."

"It was no problem. I am glad it helps. I know divorce can be hard."

June sighed softly.

"I know. I know," Lillian continued when June did not say anything. "You don't want to talk about it. I get it. I was the same way. But at some point, talking about it will help you feel better."

June struggled not to make a snarky comment about her mother's hypocrisy. "I know, Mom." Then she found herself struggling not to cry, remembering her own biological father had died. "It's just that I've got questions, you know? How could Neil have done those things to us before he left? Why not just leave? How could he even leave? How could he turn his back on his family? On me? And then start a new family—" She caught herself and quickly tried to cover. "Did he have other children? I mean, would they know about me?" She felt the tears slide down her cheeks.

"Why did it get silent?"

June instinctively walked back to the TV and saw that Mikey was no longer playing, having left his bear behind. "He snuck out of the room, probably going to sneak a cookie. I-I'm gonna let you go and go find him. Love you, Mom!" June said out of habit as she ended the call.

The first stop was the kitchen. Sure enough, she turned the corner and Mikey had opened several drawers to climb up to the countertop and the cookie jar.

"Michael P. Williams! What are you doing?" she said entering, startling the child.

He froze in place.

The sound of something metallic clanging on the counter next to her caused them both to jump. She turned to see a knife, six inches from its butcher block and at least four feet from Mikey, trembling on the countertop as if it had just been dropped.

XXIX

The Junction Falls Calvary Baptist Church was, like the town it was named after, humble. There was no stained glass on the walls to distract from the message being given, just white sheetrock. The most ornate part of the church was the pulpit. Missouri walnut panels drew attention to the mural of a cross standing tall above the American plain. The mural, painted by Michael's maternal grandmother Ruth Springer, dominated the front of the room.

The seating area faded into the background. The only objects able to compete were the two posters hanging to either side of the mural and the flags standing in either corner. The American flag was to the left. To the right was the Christian flag with its white field and blue canton, within which was a red cross, in the upper left corner.

Michael arrived two hours early to enjoy the peace—something he knew would not last long once he got home. He closed his eyes as he stood at the last pew and enjoyed the smell of the room. The pungent odor of the new carpet had finally become slightly less noticeable, and he could almost pick out the scent of old newspapers and the Bibles and hymnals in the pews. He opened his eyes and started walking toward the pulpit, his dress shoes not making a sound.

He took a seat in the front row and stared at the mural, hoping it would give him strength. "Honor thy mother and thy father" and "Thou shalt not have any gods before me" stood out. The letters were in a no-nonsense serif font, bold black against a fading white background. He hoped June would get the message if he delivered it with love.

"Please forgive me if I'm wrong," he said, not sure if he was begging for absolution from the cross or his daughter. He heard the door open.

"Dr. Reuter, I knew you'd be here early but not this early," the singsong voice of Rita Johnson interrupted his thoughts. "First sermon jitters?"

Michael stood up and smiled at the woman who'd been the church's organist since his grandmother painted that mural. "Well, first, Miss Rita, I've told you that Dr. Reuter is my wife. I'm still Michael, the kid you taught in Sunday school."

"Nonsense, Michael!" She reached up and pinched his cheek just like when he was 12. "Lillian is a pillar of the community and role model for our young women, but you have done great things, too. The least of which is getting your Doctor of Divinity."

Michael blushed.

Miss Rita paid no mind to his embarrassed silence. "Look at June and all you've done for her."

Michael looked at her, consumed with doubt. His daughter's life was a mess and, deep down, he held himself accountable. Unable to withstand Miss Rita's admiration, he averted his gaze to the deep red carpet. The old Sunday school teacher would have none of it and grabbed his jaw, making him look at her as if he were a little boy in need of guidance.

"Now you listen to me, Doctor Michael Reuter. Your June-Bug'll walk her own path and make her own mistakes. It's how God makes us grow." She looked around to make sure no other ears were present. "I should know. I was a wild child till your grandparents took me and reintroduced me to the Lord." One more shifty gaze to ensure they were alone. "There's a reason shit makes good fertilizer." She let go with a wink.

He could do nothing but smile. Sometimes God sent messages in the most unconventional—and crude—ways. One just had to listen and be open.

§

The call to prayer and the love offering were over. Michael took a deep breath as he surveyed his congregation.

"Friends, we hear a lot of ghost stories. Movies. Reality TV." He began pacing the elevated platform. "We even hear about ghosts right here in church!" His heart was pounding as he felt the spirit enter him, propelling him to speak the truth.

His gaze fell upon his daughter. June's resemblance to Lillian was showing. Her mouth was tight as she shifted in her seat, the same way she did as a child after being scolded. But the spirit was in him, guiding him.

"King Saul sought God's wisdom as he got ready to do battle against the Philistines. He could not find it in dreams or the Urim and Thummim. So, he disguised himself and went in search of any occultist who didn't leave when he drove them from his kingdom. He found an old woman, the witch of Endor, who claimed she could speak to the dead."

Michael paused and smiled. His grandson was listening with rapt attention. "Of course, she couldn't. When a person dies, his or her soul goes straight to God. There were no ghosts of believers to commune with—only demons. So, what happened? God, in his infinite wisdom, decided to show the king and the witch the folly of their ways. He sent the spirit of the prophet Samuel to advise Saul that the Philistines would defeat him in battle and that this would be his doom or his fate. When the spirit of Samuel appeared, do you know what the witch did?" He paused to scan the silent congregation.

The silence was shortly broken by Gerica's newborn who cried for a feeding.

Michael smiled warmly as his daughter's friend exited the meeting hall. As the door shut behind the young woman, he continued. "She gasped in horror!

She wasn't in control of the situation anymore. Most mediums are frauds. Using elaborate mechanisms to make it seem like there's a spirit present when there is not. Seeing an actual ghost brought back for a moment by the one, true God? This was too much for the witch of Endor. The next day, Saul was defeated and committed suicide.

"The lesson God is teaching the witch, Saul, and us is that faith is a currency. Like money, we can save it and spend it wisely. For our spiritual currency, this means spending it all on God. To turn to *Him* during times of trouble. However, when we turn to false idols to solve our problems, such as celebrities, politicians, or modern witches of Endor, we are misspending our spiritual dollars. When we do this, God will know. God will, out of love, bring us low to see the error of our ways." Michael's eyes met June's; she looked angry and, if Michael didn't know better, guilty of something. He suppressed a self-satisfied grin.

It was tough love, and he hated to see her squirm uncomfortably, but he knew the message had been received.

XXX

"As he was calling you 'The Witch of Endor,' I knew I just *had* to come over after church, but Michael insisted on a celebratory lunch and I couldn't get away until today," June said, laughing as she sipped honeyed Earl Grey and relaxed with Sara-Lyn. "Gerica took Mikey on a playdate and I didn't have classes today, so I called you."

"It's okay. I'm used to being called such things." Sara-Lyn took the last sip of her tea and placed the cup in its saucer. "Have you been meditating?"

"I have!" June took out her phone and tried to pull up YouTube, frowning when she couldn't get a signal. "I was going to show you this YouTube channel I found. It has this haunting instrumental music that's helped me focus and open my mind. Ever try anything like that?"

"Music can be powerful." Sara-Lyn nodded. "Perhaps I have something on a CD downstairs we can listen to?"

§

Sara-Lyn found her *Gifts of the Angels* CD by Steven Halpern. "I've been listening to him since the '70s."

The music started off sounding like a choir of angels. The two women sat down in a cross-legged pose, their upturned hands on their knees. Sara-Lyn kept her eyes closed, and June concentrated on the clear quartz. Soon June's mind was clear, and she felt at peace. She closed her eyes.

June saw herself in a mirror dressed in white. She was not in a room but in a space of nothing but a bright white. She could hear what sounded like many voices all trying to speak at once, but they were not loud. They then became silent, and she no longer felt alone. June turned to look over her shoulder and saw the albino stag sauntering toward her.

She felt joy at seeing him. "Hello, old friend."

"Greetings, sister of The Circle," the deer responded. In a pulsing light, he transformed into a very old man. "It is good you can hear me now. Took you long enough." His tone was full of mirth.

"You are *real."*

"I am. But you are disappointed that I'm the one who came through."

His words caused June to look away in shame.

"It's all right. You were hoping for your father."

"I'm sorry."

He laughed. "No, you're not. Maybe you're sorry that I'll be offended, but you're not sorry that you're disappointed. It's

218

only natural that a child's soul cries for her parent. There is no reason I should be offended that he is who you seek."

"Is he here?"

The man nodded. "He has a path he must walk now. Once he gets it sorted in his soul, he'll understand his purpose. Then he'll reveal himself to you."

June felt comforted by the man's words. "Who are you?"

"My name is Wahchinksapa. My tribe shares your land."

June looked confused. "I've never seen a Native American near our house."

He smiled his broad grin. "Young sister of The Circle, time and space are relative. At least, those are the words your people use. You and I share the same space, just not at the same time. Some are gifted with the blessing to peek behind the veil. The river of time shares a few of her secrets with us." He placed a hand on her shoulder. "I must go now. When your lifeblood is bleeding out, go to The Circle. I have already covered you." He turned and, in the same light that transformed him from deer to man, walked away.

"What does that even mean?" she shouted as his form blended with the rest of the spirit world. He was gone.

§

"It makes sense," Sara-Lyn said after June recounted her experience. "We experience time in a linear fashion, but really, reality is happening all at the same time. Any luck on the name search?"

"No," June said, her attention focused on the screen of her phone as she searched with a newly found signal for any record of the man she had just met. "All I can find is that his name means 'wise.'" Her shoulders fell in frustration.

"I didn't think you would. However, I've been doing some research of my own." Sara-Lyn stood and shuffled through some papers on a nearby end table. Returning to June, she took a deep breath. "I've got an admission to make. I did a little trespassing at your place on Sunday."

"You did? Why didn't you ask me?" June looked shocked but not upset.

"Knowing Michael like I do, I didn't want to put you in the position of either having to ask or having to lie, but I just couldn't resist seeing it for myself and testing my theory that it's a nexus between ley lines."

June looked away thoughtfully. "That was probably wise. Thank you."

"Anyway, I don't think you're dealing with just one haunting. A place like yours that's been around for a while has history. There have been at least two deaths at the site since the armory was built in 1877. One was a suicide during the Spanish-American War. Another was a young girl getting a clandestine abortion during prohibition."

"Really? Three ghosts?" June said, stunned.

"Maybe more. Legend holds it that a Jayhawk raid from Kansas killed the first white settler on the land. Before that, the Missouria tribe was known to migrate through the area. If it's a powerful nexus like I think it is, a powerful medicine man's spirit would be drawn to the place."

"Medicine man? Don't you think that's a little … cliché?" June asked, raising an eyebrow.

"No. First, we're not dealing with an angry spirit like in the movies. This spirit sees something in you from across time. Something that transcends our physical reality. Secondly, that he can take the form of an animal suggests he has power." Sara-Lyn sipped her second cup of Earl Grey.

June looked at the older woman with a mix of awe and doubt. "How do you know so much?"

Sara-Lyn laughed in her distinct giggle. "Honey, I'm a flower child from the '60s and '70s. Mr. Pocaro's work in concert lighting allowed us the freedom to travel and meet some very interesting people. I've met the second most powerful voodoo priest in Haiti, meditated in a Buddhist nunnery in South Korea, and learned from a Sioux medicine man. I even went on a vision quest complete with peyote."

"It's hard to believe anyone could do that in one lifetime," June said, feeling the weight of single motherhood and looming student loans.

"You have a rough path ahead of you, but I have faith that you'll make it through." Sara-Lyn placed a soothing hand on June's knee, as she was wont to do these days. "But you need to know all the barriers in your way. I think I'm correct about your home sitting on the intersection of ley lines and being a nexus point. It's attracting powerful forces."

"Like Wahchinksapa?"

"Yes, but not only from the light. There are dark forces at play, too. In what must be the spot you and Wahchinksapa call The Circle, I was at peace. By the tree, I could tell that there was a balance between good and evil, but I was still safe. However, I tried looking into your basement, and it was there something attacked me."

"Physically?" June asked.

"At first, I thought so. I heard a gunshot as if someone were standing in front of me, executing me. I even felt the bullet tear into me, but I was the only one there. I saw a face in the window." Sara-Lyn shuddered at the memory. "It made me look into what could be there other than ghosts."

"What did you find?"

"Well, in Western traditions, there are poltergeists. In India, there is the *pishacha* that feeds off human emotion and creates what one most craves. In Korea, the *dokkaebi* are goblins or spirits that interact with humans for good or bad, depending on how they are treated. In most cases, these spirits feed off of or react to negative emotions."

June stared into space, taking in Sara-Lyn's words. "Do you think it's the *dokkaebi* because we're Korean?"

Sara-Lyn shook her head. "You have good instincts. I wanted to look into Korean spirituality because darkness can follow a person. Many cultures have traditions of curses that are passed down from generation to generation. I thought maybe that could be what's going on here." She sipped her tea. "But I don't think so. I meditated on the attack and the entity behind it is tied to the land, not a person."

"So, it's angry we're in its home?" June asked.

"No, the opposite actually. If it's inhuman, it probably needs people living there to feed off of. Since it's an entity of the dark, it's going to feed off the negativity of the people living there. In fact, it could be instigating conflict to produce more anger and resentment to feed its insatiable appetite."

June took a deep breath. "Could a spirit push someone to commit murder?"

Sara-Lyn looked her student in the eyes. "In extreme cases. People have used the defense of being possessed throughout history. Modern science tells us it's a mental illness. And in most cases, it probably is. However, you and I can see beyond the veil that separates worlds. We know that some things defy science. And some people defy reason."

A tear slid down June's cheek. "Maybe. I don't want to even think it's true. Mom saves lives. She's a hero. All Emily gave me was circumstantial evidence."

Sara-Lyn gave her best impartial sigh. "It's an extreme possibility but a possibility nonetheless."

June looked at her phone. "Crap. I'm late for dinner. I'm surprised Michael hasn't called already." She wiped another tear from her eye.

"Are you okay to drive?"

"Yeah, I think so. Just got to have an alibi ready for

when I get home. The later I stay, the more I'm going to have to explain."

§

As a man of God, Michael often had a sense when something was off. When June was 17 and had just gotten her driver's license, he awoke from a dead sleep. Minutes later, she called him and said she had swerved to miss a dog and went into a ditch. He had the same feeling tonight.

XXXI

As Lillian parked outside of her house, pleasant memories of coming home from trips like this one brought a smile to her face. She would often enter the kitchen and see her daughter and husband engaged in deep discussion over her homeschool studies. Philosophy, politics, and economics were recurring themes of heated debate. Math and the hard sciences, to her disappointment, did not enliven her family's intellectual discussions.

As she got out of her car, the weight of the news she had to break weighed on her. June would get upset. There would be some screaming, and her daughter would show her ugly side. But in the end, Lillian knew she would make everything better. She would console June, and life would return to normal. She placed her hand on the doorknob to enter the house.

Neither Michael nor June heard her enter over their screaming at each other. Michael's booming voice was the first she could understand.

"I told you—begged you—not to see that-that *witch*!" he growled. "What do I need to do? Forbid it?"

"I'm not a kid anymore!" June shouted back. "I can go where I want and hang out with whomever I want! I do *not* need your permission!"

Lillian slipped into the kitchen and put her purse down. "What's going on?"

Her daughter and husband turned to look at her, speaking at the same time.

"Your husband wants to control me!"

"Your daughter is hanging out with a literal witch!"

"Slow down. One at a time. June, did you go see Pocaro again?" she asked.

"Yes." June crossed her arms across her chest. "I'm a grown woman who will do what she wants."

"You're a grown woman living in *my* house," Michael shot back, also crossing his arms. "A house of God. And you will obey *His* rules if not mine."

"Are we so arrogant that we know all that God allows? Just because we memorize a book written by imperfect men?" June fired back.

"Blasphemy!" Michael roared.

"What would you call it, Mom? You always taught me to use my head and think for myself."

"I would call it critical thinking," Lillian said in a soft, calm tone.

Michael's irritation did not go unnoticed.

"It's also disrespectful," Lillian continued. "You know our beliefs. I can't stop you from doubting them, but please don't bring that doubt into this house."

June rolled her eyes, turned, and walked out of the room.

"That went well," Lillian said, turning her attention to her husband.

"Always." Michael shook his head as he began talking. "Always taking her side. A little nod to me at the end but nothing substantial. A slap-on-the-wrist lecture about disrespect and you let her do whatever. It gets old. And I feel like you have her back more than mine, but we've had this argument before. We've had this argument before in this kitchen!"

Lillian stepped toward the fridge.

"Not this time," Michael said, leaning on the door. "Not this time." He turned and left the room before Lillian could speak.

XXXII

June thrashed as she tried to sleep. She rolled over and stared at the ceiling. She was still fully awake. Her mind was reeling from the past few weeks. For the first time in her life, someone believed her "crazy" stories about spirits. Sara-Lyn had also taught June about her own abilities, allowing her to feel a powerful connection to an unseen reality. However, Michael saw anything to do with Sara-Lyn as blasphemous and her mother thought her beliefs ludicrous.

Then she heard it—the familiar knocking that seemed to come from inside the walls. June now knew this was not Wahchinksapa or another benevolent spirit. This was evil.

"Knock it off!" she said angrily. "I just want to fuckin' sleep." But this time, she did not whimper. June controlled her rage and did not surrender it to this spirit. "I don't know why you hate me, but it stops—now."

In response, a framed picture of her with Mikey and her parents flew off the wall to the other side of the room, the glass shattering on impact. June sat upright in bed and stared wide-eyed at the destruction. She bolted out of her room, the door slamming shut behind her. She made her way directly to Mikey's room only for his door to slam shut in her face. She tried the knob, but it would not turn. She knew the only lock was a slide lock on the inside of the door. She knew it was too high for him to reach.

She put her shoulder into it, but the door wouldn't budge. She hit it again with all her might, but nothing was working. She finally paused to listen. She heard neither terrified wailing nor the panicked sound of her parents hurrying to see what the problem was. Her mind began questioning whether she was dreaming.

June's bedroom door suddenly reopened. She entered the room with the intent to crawl back into bed and dismiss it all as a walking nightmare. The twinkling of glass on the floor caught her eye. The photo collage still lay in a crumpled mess in the blue light of the moon. Then she heard it again.

"No." June's voice took an icy tone. "No more." Defiant tears slid down her cheeks as a sense of control replaced her more familiar fear. "I *am* going to sleep tonight."

§

Her bare feet seemed to levitate as she walked toward the kitchen. Michael's recent sage harvest had been large, and he would not miss a bundle if she burned it.

But as she rounded the corner, she was met with the loud banging of drawers opening and closing. She had stood up to the knocking, but this reignited her fear.

She began to cry as she noticed the large chef's knife extract itself from the butcher's block. It slowly turned until it was pointing directly at her. She stood, teary-eyed and transfixed, as it floated gently upward before rapidly flinging itself in her direction. She raised her hands defensively as she twisted out of its path. June felt the blade make brief contact with her right wrist before it stuck into the wall behind her.

She looked down and saw the trickle of blood forming at the neat new slit. She felt the sting of the cut. She felt a sudden oppressive need to get out of the house. She bolted for the back door, grabbing a kitchen towel as she ran. The banging of cabinet doors and drawers mocked her as she fled. Whatever just happened was stronger than her and knew it.

Her bare feet, kissed by the spring dew, moved on instinct. She wrapped her injured wrist in the towel. Suddenly, June realized she had left her child in that house. She was a terrible mother. She kept running. She was a terrible mother, and she had been a terrible child, and she felt like that child all over again.

Finally regaining some control over her body, she collapsed, sobbing, and clawed at the grass as she turned to face the house. It was then she realized where she was. She'd made it to The Circle. As if emerging from underwater, June began to feel calm. She focused on the things Sara-Lyn had been teaching her.

Some spirits preyed upon the insecurities of their victims. She had to tell herself she had not been a bad mother by leaving Mikey behind. *I removed the danger by removing myself.* She managed to take a deep breath, feeling The Circle reinforce her will. She looked around the familiar place and began to smile. This place had to hold some answers—a way to fight.

But not tonight.

Exhaustion was setting in. As her eyes fluttered closed, she could barely make out the movement behind the old oak tree. A face with sad eyes stared back at her.

§

Michael woke before the rest of the house, which was typical for a Saturday morning. He slipped out of bed, taking care not to disturb his slumbering wife. It was too early to think too much about whatever the day held for them. He needed coffee, so he headed to the kitchen.

He noticed June's door was open a crack. He knocked before slowly opening it to see what she wanted for breakfast. His heart skipped a beat as he saw the bed in disarray and the missing photo from above her headboard. A quick scan of the room revealed the missing frame on the floor.

"Lillian!" he shouted as he left the doorway and ran downstairs.

That's where he saw a knife stuck in the wall. "What the hell?" He looked in the kitchen and saw various drawers and doors open, their contents jumbled and tossed about the kitchen. He heard his wife bounding down the stairs.

"What's going on?" Lillian asked as she saw the kitchen for the first time. "What the fuck happened here?"

"I don't know. It looks like June's room has been ransacked, and she's not in there."

"Where is she?" she asked, her voice tinged with worry.

"I don't know." He looked at the door leading outside. "I'm checking outside. Why don't you check on Mikey?" He started moving outside as Lillian headed to check on their grandson.

He saw her still form lying on the grass. He started running and slid next to her like a baseball player taking home plate.

"June!" he yelled. He took her into his arms and saw the kitchen towel wrapped around her wrist and the blood soaked through it. "JUNE!" he screamed again, fearing the worst.

June stirred in his arms, and her eyes blinked open. "Daddy?" she asked, her voice soft and heavy with sleep. "I-I'm all right. I was-I was … just sleeping."

"What the hell is going on?" Lillian yelled as she ran toward them.

Michael lifted June's wrist with the towel wrapped around it.

"Not again," she said as she dropped to her knees and pulled June from Michael's embrace. "Fuck this place," she hissed.

"No," June said softly. "It's not what it looks like. It's not what you think."

"What the hell is it then?" Lillian grilled, her rage intensifying.

"You're not going to believe me."

"Try us," Michael said in a soft, sympathetic tone.

She closed her eyes. "I was trying to sleep, but the knocking came back and woke me up, and it wouldn't let me go back to sleep."

"So, you broke the picture frame?" he asked her.

"No, it just flew off on its own," June explained.

Lillian scoffed. "Did the knife just stick itself in the wall as well?"

"If you must know," she said as confidently as the blood loss would allow, "yes."

"Honey," Lillian growled. "Ghosts are not real!" She clasped June's bandaged wrist. "We have been through this before. Remember when you were 16?"

"No!" June struggled to protest. "This is nothing like that! I'm telling you the truth!"

PART THREE:
A Home in Disorder

Love is patient, love is kind. It is not jealous, is not pompous, it is not inflated, it is not rude, it does not seek its own interests, it is not quick-tempered, it does not brood over injury, it does not rejoice over wrongdoing but rejoices with the truth. It bears all things, believes all things, hopes all things, endures all things.

Love never fails. If there are prophecies, they will be brought to nothing; if tongues, they will cease; if knowledge, it will be brought to nothing. For we know partially and we prophesy partially, but when the perfect comes, the partial will pass away.

When I was a child, I used to talk as a child, think as a child, reason as a child; when I became a man, I put aside childish things. At present we see indistinctly, as in a mirror, but then face to face. At present I know partially; then I shall know fully, as I am fully known. So faith, hope, love remain, these three; but the greatest of these is love.

— 1 Corinthians 13:4-13 (New Revised Standard Version, Catholic Edition)

XXXIII

"Lillian, I did not expect to see you here today," a voice boomed from behind her. "When I heard the call, I assumed you would call in sick."

She turned and looked up at the chief of emergency medicine, a forlorn look on her face. This was one of the drawbacks of working in the ER of a rural hospital: Everyone knew when you or your family had an emergency.

"I thought about it, but my choices were work or stay home and fail at distracting myself."

He nodded knowingly, having worked with Lillian for almost 15 years. She did the same thing when June had attempted suicide the last time.

"I don't know how you do it—balancing being an amazing mother and gifted physician. I know I could never do it with your grace."

She beamed at the compliment, her mood instantly picking up. "Thank you, Ajit. It is draining, but I just do what needs to be done."

"Well, just let me know. And we can change the schedule if you need to take time," he said as he started moving off to finish his rounds.

§

June stared over the shoulder of Dr. Derek Wackerfuss as he tried to figure out how she got the cut.

"It's been eight years since we last met in this office," he said softly. "I believe it was for similar reasons. Please, tell me what happened." His voice had the practiced soothing quality stereotypical of a therapist.

"You wouldn't believe it," she said as she tried to make herself look as small as possible in her seat. She wore the scrubs she had been given when she was brought in.

Wackerfuss smiled his warm, comforting smile. "You know me. We've sat in this office before."

His office was in the Wyldewood Behavioral Health Center just south of Kansas City. She was hospitalized at this facility for a week when she was a teenager. She looked at him, remaining silent.

"Is it the ghosts? Have they returned?"

She looked down, picking at her fingernails. It had been a very long day, and it was only 2:00 p.m. The ambulance had taken her from their home to the emergency room. She stayed in the secure emergency psychiatry area for several hours as a team of doctors and social workers evaluated her.

June answered the same question posed in multiple forms by all of them: "Are you thinking of hurting yourself or others?" Each time she answered with a firm no. They analyzed the cut on her wrist and determined it was too dangerous to release her. She was then transferred to this facility.

"Your report says," he picked up the report for effect, "you've been speaking with a medium who confirmed the existence of several of the spirits you claim you've encountered at your home. I seem to remember that you, like many highly intelligent creatives, have an affinity for magical thinking."

She rolled her eyes.

He adopted a more prodding, adversarial tone. "Have you considered that maybe this medium shares this affinity?"

"You sound like my mother," she blurted out.

She chided herself, knowing that her wall of defiance had cracked just a little. This was not her first rodeo, and she knew he would eventually break down the wall. She looked up, meeting his gaze. If she was going to talk, it would be on her terms and not his.

"I woke up to knocking. A picture frame from above my bed flew, by itself, across the room. I went downstairs, and I saw doors and drawers opening and closing by themselves. A knife flew across the room, cutting me. But I guess these things were all in my head." Her tone was sardonic, challenging him for a logical explanation as she waved her bandaged arm for effect.

"They may all be in your head, but this does not mean you are crazy." His voice was once again soothing. "You were in bed, so you could have been in that transition zone between wakefulness and sleep. You could have been doing these things while you were dreaming. Some of these other things could have been some sort of dissociative state, a defense mechanism considering all the stress you have been dealing with."

June had to admit that those explanations did sound logical and were comforting. They would mean there was not some evil or malevolent force harassing and attacking her. The theories Wackerfuss postulated also implied that she was sane. She wanted to embrace them enthusiastically and just walk out of the facility, but she'd been told that she'd be here for at least 72 hours.

"Look, Doc, I have been under a lot of stress lately. And yes, I have been feeling depressed. I married a man I thought I could build a comfortable life with. When he could not keep it in his pants, that delusion ended. Now I've had to drop out of one college and transfer to another as a single mother. I moved back in with my parents because I cannot support myself or my son." She reached for a cup of water with her bandaged hand.

"June, how are things at home? Do you feel safe?"

The change in conversation caught her by surprise. "Yes," she said in a slow, measured tone. "Why wouldn't I feel safe?"

"Oh, no reason. Just a standard question I have to ask." He made another note.

"My relationship with my parents is fine. I mean, my mom does get on my nerves at times. I don't think she has fully come to terms with the fact that I'm an adult now. I have a child, yet she still lectures me if I stay out too late. She feels like she can boss me around like when I was a kid. There are some conflicts, mostly about my desire to have gotten to know my biological father."

"How upset does she get?"

Another deep sigh. "She shuts down the conversation. She uses a guilt trip. I mean, the guy was a piece of shit. He was abusive and abandoned us when we needed him the most. So, I get it. I would have probably been severely disappointed had I met him. But hey, she only refused me for my own good, right? Not that it matters now."

The psychologist made a few more notes. "Nothing violent?"

"No."

"What about your stepfather?"

She chortled at the thought of Michael being violent. "He does not have a mean or violent bone in his body. This is a man who gave up his career to homeschool me. He gets angry when it comes to matters of the soul, but that's only because he cares."

He crossed out a note. "Now, if I remember correctly from when you were 16, you were brought in here with several cuts. This time there is only one cut. Why did you stop at the first one?"

She frowned and awkwardly covered her wrist with her left hand. "I didn't try to kill myself this time." Her voice conveyed veracious sincerity.

He paused, studying her face and examining her expression. "Last time, this was over a boy, a friend, and bullying." His eyes took in her reaction.

She winced at the painful memory. "Ouch, but that's in the past. I'm beyond caring what people say about me."

"What about this time? Are you seeing anyone at the moment?"

"No."

He crossed out another note. "Well, your father dropped off a suitcase of your clothes and some toiletries. I imagine you would like a shower?"

"That would be nice," she replied, her voice heavy with emotional exhaustion. "I guess I couldn't call home? My son must be worried sick. Please just let me tell him I'm safe." A tear slid down her cheek.

Against the facility's policy, he picked up the phone and dialed a number. Moments later, a female orderly knocked and entered his office.

"Kira here will help you get your things and show you to your room. Then she will let you use the phone."

XXXIV

Throwing herself into work only helped for so long. Lillian had to come home sometime and deal with the fact that her daughter had once again tried to kill herself.

She lingered in the basement after bringing yet another box from June's room to store in the comforting darkness until they could donate it or hold a yard sale. When June left for college, they never did anything with her room, opting to leave it frozen in time so the sense of nostalgia would continue calling her back home. While tidying up after the mess June left behind, Lillian decided it was time to redecorate. It would be a nice surprise for when her daughter was released from this round of hospitalization. It would help her heal and move on.

"This was a good idea," she mumbled into the darkest corner of the basement.

Reentering June's room, she cut her foot on a piece of shattered glass. She watched the blood run down the jagged slash in her arch. The sight didn't bother her, nor did gore. Dissection had been her favorite activity in the anatomy and biology courses she took through high school and medical school. She smirked as she remembered taking a friend into the "gross" anatomy lab and how he still insists he blocked the sight from memory.

Still, she had to stop the bleeding. She stepped into June's bathroom and washed the cut thoroughly. It was just deep enough that stitches were an option but not a requirement. She bandaged it up and turned off the lights. A blue blur caught her eye as she passed Mikey's room. The sight of the bear made her smile. When Mikey outgrew it, the toy would not be relegated to a box in the basement. Instead, she would give it a place of honor in her study. Family and visitors would recognize it as a treasured memento from her grandchild's youth. But she would know the truth.

Lillian resumed the chore of cleaning up her daughter's messes. She stopped tossing items into boxes to sweep up the glass, cursing herself for not doing it first. Yet despite the dull ache in her foot, she hummed.

Lillian had never minded a mother's duty to be tormented by her children. It was not all bad. While June could be difficult, she was grateful more often than not. However, June's refusal to let the sperm donor remain in the past changed that. While satisfying, killing Neil had not been what she wanted. It was something she *had* to do—was *forced* to do—because of June.

Lillian frowned, her fingers lingering on June's laptop. The girl did have a history of chronic illness. While seemingly in remission, it could worsen at any time. And June's history of self-mutilation and suicide attempts made her being successful the next time believable. The offending laptop was something she could justify keeping for herself if June took a turn for the worse. But Lillian's thoughts then turned to June's journal. A daughter's thoughts would be something a grieving mother who had sacrificed so much for the good of her child should treasure. While some would consider displaying it macabre, it would not be too far from normal.

Lillian's gaze next fell upon a stuffed lamb with fleece far from white as snow. "Buttercup" had been June's first toy, a gift from Charlie and an instant delight for the infant. It had sat atop a pile of stuff marked for storage, but she decided to set it aside instead.

§

The warm shower filled the room with steam as it washed the day's labors from Lillian's skin. She closed her eyes and felt the warm water on her face and running through her hair. She spat some out as she turned to feel the sensation on her back. She practiced some breathing techniques.

It bothered her that June still believed in the childish notions of ghosts and mediums. June believed in them so completely that she was okay with going behind her parents' backs to visit some crazy woman deep in the woods. She shook her head dismissively as she rinsed the last bit of shampoo from her hair. Bending over, she turned off the water before reaching for her oversized towel. After wrapping her hair, she reached for another, pulling the shower curtain back. She froze, her breath caught in her throat.

There on the bathroom mirror, written in a strange hand, was one word: TRUTH.

XXXV

June had been in the facility for the full 72 hours and was looking forward to going home. She had slept well the night before, better than she had in several months. Even food tasted better than it had in a while. Refreshed, she looked forward to playing and snuggling with Mikey, who she had not seen since she left in an ambulance. There had been some quick phone calls but nothing more. It was just her mother or father who had visited her; Lillian argued that it would not be good for the boy to see his mother "locked away."

She did one more sweep of her room for anything left behind and then zipped her small suitcase. There was a knock at her open door, and she turned to see Kira standing there.

"Your parents are here."

She smiled. "Thank you, Kira."

"Good luck," the woman said as she escorted June to the front of the facility.

§

Michael had spent the last three days on his knees, praying for his daughter. It was just like when she was 16 and spent a week in the very facility he was now pulling up to. This time he and his wife had gotten the call that his prayers had been answered: June was going to be released after 72 hours. Holding hands, he and Lillian entered the hospital.

He stood back and let his wife handle the paper-work and gave mother and daughter some space as June emerged. She was escorted by Dr. Wackerfuss, who stepped next to Michael.

"Mr. Reuter," he said, shaking Michael's hand. "Can I speak to you for a moment?"

"Sure," Michael replied.

"I don't think she was suicidal," Dr. Wackerfuss began. "In my opinion, your daughter was having some sort of waking dream coupled with sleepwalking. She may also be experiencing some PTSD. Are you sure no one else was in the house that night?"

Michael's expression became one of confused concern. "I'm fairly sure. Why?"

Dr. Wackerfuss let out a sigh. "Her wound is on the wrist of her dominant hand, and there is only one. It is light like a hesitancy cut, as in what we would expect if she were getting her courage up to kill herself. But we would have seen more of them." He paused, realizing who he was speaking to. "I'm sorry. I forgot you probably know better than anyone what I'm talking about."

Michael nodded solemnly. "So, I take it you think it was different this time?"

"Yes. I think they may be defensive in nature."

A visible chill went through Michael. "Are you saying someone attacked her? Did this to her?" As the words came out, he started becoming angry.

"It is a possibility but not the only one. I'm just trying to wrap my head around what happened to her."

"As are we."

"There is another thing. She believes this is the result of the supernatural." As Dr. Wackerfuss spoke, Michael nodded in acknowledgment. "So, one thing that may help—and this sounds radical—is perhaps a ritual of some sort."

Michael raised his eyebrow, dubious of the suggestion.

"A religious one like an exorcism."

"I had been thinking of contacting a friend of mine who is a Catholic priest," Michael responded as he considered the suggestion. "I was nervous about confirming what we consider to be a delusion."

"Makes sense," the doctor conceded. "But in this case, it could put her mind at ease."

"I'll talk it over with Lillian." He shook the doctor's hand and then rejoined his family.

"What did Wackerfuss want?" Lillian asked.

"Can we talk about it later?"

She looked at him intently. "If it's something medical, I would like to know right now, Michael Reuter. What if whatever it is leaves me with questions for him? I would like to ask them while I have the chance."

He sighed. June looked away like she always did when she sensed a fight was about to break out between her parents.

"He recommended that we have someone come in and do a religious ritual. It could help reduce anxiety."

Lillian pursed her lips and tilted her head before shaking it in disbelief. "Has everyone boarded the supernatural crazy train?" She threw up her hands. "All of this modern medicine and we are just going to revert to superstition and ritual?" She looked at her daughter. "Fine. Whatever. Let's go home." She started walking toward the car.

Father and daughter shared a conspiratorial look.

June mouthed "Thank you."

Michael nodded and hugged her. "This will be done in a Christian manner. I'll reach out to my Catholic friend. I don't want Sara-Lyn involved," he whispered.

"Okay," she whispered back.

§

"Mommy will be home soon," Mikey said to his teddy bear while he rolled his trucks, his babysitter in another room. He stopped and looked at the stuffed animal. "I want Mommy, too. I love Mommy, too." He giggled.

"That's funny." He went over and hugged the bear. "I love you, too."

§

After dinner, all Mikey wanted was to cuddle with June and watch *The Lion King*.

"June, before you go be with your son, come," Lillian said as she grabbed her daughter's hand and led her upstairs.

"Where are you taking me?" June asked as Mikey and Michael left to start the movie.

"I have a surprise for you." Lillian grinned as she led her daughter into her newly redecorated bedroom.

The walls had been repainted in the medium, neutral green of matcha tea leaves. The old furniture had been replaced by a shiplap-inspired panel bed in a white finish. In a place of honor on the bed sat Buttercup the lamb. A matching dresser and nightstand, each with distressed wood tops, completed the look.

"Whoa," June said as she entered her room. "I was thinking about doing this but didn't know how you'd feel about it. I love this color!"

"I was worried you'd be upset I'd changed your room. Wait until you see the walls in the daylight. The paint seems to change with the sun," Lillian said, trying to hide her dislike of the color. It reminded her of grass, which made her feet itch.

"Buttercup!" June squealed. She scooped the stuffed animal off the bed, holding it to her chest. "I'll have to show Mikey!"

"Maybe she and his bear can have a playdate?" Lillian suggested.

"I love you, Mom!" June turned and hugged Lillian with a tear sliding down her cheek.

"And I love you," Lillian said. "Now, I know how sudden and unexpected separations from your child can be hard. Go. Enjoy your son."

"Thank you." She paused, a thoughtful expression on her face. "And something else I'm thankful for." June gave her another squeeze. "Thank you for agreeing to the exorcism."

Lillian hugged her daughter back. "It's okay, sweet pea. I just get frustrated sometimes. I don't want to waste time on the ancient rituals of a denomination I don't believe in. I think medically, and I want to find an effective solution. Anything less," Lillian met her daughter's eyes, "frustrates me. I only care about your health. But if this has some sort of psychological effect and helps you, I'm all for it."

June pulled away. "I know that, Mom. Which is why I want to thank you for letting us try it anyway."

It was Lillian's turn to give June a hug. "I love you."

"I love you, too."

§

Mikey had barely made it halfway through the movie before passing out. June soon followed her son's lead. She awoke as the credits were ending, a fleece lovingly placed over mother and son by her father. She checked her phone: It was 11:24 p.m. She was tired.

She turned off the TV and lifted Mikey with a slight grunt. She would not be carrying him around much longer. Quietly, she made it through the darkened house to his bedroom. After laying him down, she crawled into the bed herself—she needed to hold him. She had thought about sleeping in her room.

Too soon.

Her eyelids became heavy, and she drifted to sleep.

§

She awoke, staring up at a ceiling painted blue by the moonlight. It was like she had gone from sleep to full consciousness in an instant, sensing that she and Mikey were not alone. She reached for her phone: 3:01 a.m. Then she thought she felt the bed move. She looked down toward the source of the movement.

All she saw was Mikey's blue and white bear.

"I have got to be dreaming," she said out loud as she tried to kick the creepy toy off the bed.

But she could not move.

And she could swear the tiny head cocked to the side.

And as if on cue, she fainted.

XXXVI

When one ran a parish in a sparsely populated area, it was not unusual to get a call for spiritual help from other religious leaders. Sure, not everyone had enough of an open mind and heart to seek out the aid of others who did not walk the same path to Christ. That Michael Reuter did have such an open mind did not surprise Father Nicholas Campbell. What did surprise him was his friend's admission that his daughter had been working with a local medium behind his back.

The two had met at a prayer breakfast after Michael's congregation had been rocked by a sex scandal—a youth pastor had been sleeping with several underage girls, two having become pregnant. The two men talked about how the news of these types of scandals can rock one's faith to its core. The Catholic priest and the Baptist lay minister quickly became friends. When Michael called to ask for a house blessing, Father Campbell did not hesitate to oblige.

He pulled up and stepped out of his car. He smiled at the innocent sight of June and her son playing in the yard.

"Hi, Father Campbell." She waved, happy to see him.

Mikey looked at the priest, confused. "He's not your daddy, Mommy."

"It's what people call priests. They are kinda like the pastor at church."

Mikey looked at the priest, cocking his head. Satisfied with whatever childish conclusion he arrived at, he shrugged his shoulders and went back to playing.

"Let's take this inside, Mikey. I'll put a movie on for you," June said just as he was about to scamper off after a blue-tailed skink.

Forgetting the lizard, he grabbed his bear and ran inside.

"Come, Father. Mom and Dad are waiting for you inside."

"Nick!" Michael said, greeting him at the door. "Thank you for doing this."

"Anytime for you, my friend."

"Shall we have some lunch?" Michael asked. "You said on the phone you wanted to talk to us about what's been going on."

"Breaking bread is never a bad way to talk about spiritual matters. Especially when that bread is made by such an excellent chef as you."

Michael blushed at the generous compliment. The men entered the kitchen and took a seat at the table in the breakfast nook. Lillian and June had set the table and plated servings of Michael's famous salt-baked lamb and potato rissoles.

"Father," Lillian, ever the gracious hostess, said in a sweet tone, "as our guest, would you like to say grace?"

"Thank you, Lillian." He placed his hands together, and his hosts held hands. "Bless us, O Lord, and these Thy gifts, which we are about to receive from Thy bounty. Through Christ, Our Lord, Amen."

"Amen," the three Baptists echoed as he made the sign of the cross.

He took the first bite and closed his eyes in epicurean delight. "Mmm, fantastic as always, Michael."

"Thank you" was his humble reply.

Father Campbell turned to June. "So, Michael told me all that's happened—that you were experiencing some pretty unnatural occurrences. You've even been talking to Sara-Lyn Pocaro. Is this true?"

June pushed some food around on her plate with her eyes downcast as she gathered the courage to speak. "Yes," she finally said.

"Has she been in the house? Could she have brought something in with her?" Lillian asked.

"Mom," June answered, "I know what lines not to cross."

"What about things like Tarot cards?" Michael interjected. "Other things she could've given June that she brought into the house? Could they have brought evil with them?"

The priest took a deep breath, considering it. "It is possible. It is also possible that she stirred up things that were already here. I understand that you, June, have believed there were ghosts the entire time you have lived here. Is this true?"

"Yes, sir," came her soft reply. "Trust me, I don't want to."

"What exactly does the Catholic Church believe about ghosts, Father?" Lillian asked.

"Well, simply, if, for whatever reason, God wills that a spirit should linger, it is possible. However, these cases are exceptionally rare. Mostly it is something going on medically or psychologically. But when it's the case of something truly supernatural, it's usually a demon at work."

"Can things or places become possessed?" Michael asked.

The priest took a bite and pondered the question. "Depends on who you ask. Some say yes, things can be possessed. Others call it an infestation. As for me, I'm more of a pragmatist. What you call it matters less than the need to cleanse the person, place, or thing."

"So, you can perform an exorcism on a house?" June asked, warming to the conversation as it more definitively steered away from blaming her.

The priest chuckled. "You could say that. We call it a house blessing. I came prepared to do one. I even brought cheat sheets so you can follow along."

"After lunch," Lillian said, setting the schedule.

"That sounds great to me," he agreed.

"Father?" June asked, her voice trembling nervously. "There's been some talk that I," she hesitated, "might be a medium. Does that mean I'm possessed or that something is wrong with me?"

"No, child," he said, finishing a bite. "There are mystics in the Catholic Church. Many have even become saints. The trick, though, is knowing when it is from Heaven and when it is from elsewhere. The Catholic Church is unique in that we have a system for such things. I don't want you to think I'm proselytizing here."

Michael nodded that he was okay—so far. His gaze lingered on Lillian who finally nodded.

"We believe in the supernatural in that its existence comes from God's will," he continued. "So, when we have someone who demonstrates these kinds of gifts, we train them the best we can to separate the Divine from the demonic. This can only be accomplished if the mystic is totally obedient to God and the teachings of the Holy Mother Church."

§

After lunch, Father Campbell retrieved a case from his car. He handed the scripts to the adults as Mikey watched his movie. Lillian, June, and Michael read over the prayers and responses expected of them while he put on his vestments.

"Okay, shall we begin here in the kitchen?"

The family nodded in agreement.

"In the name of the Father, and of the Son, and of the Holy Spirit," he began.

"Amen," the three responded in unison.

"Peace be to this house and to all who dwell here, in the name of the Lord."

"Blessed be God forever." The family shared slightly uncomfortable looks between them.

"When Christ took flesh through the Blessed Virgin Mary, he made his home with us. Let us now pray that he will enter this home and bless it with his presence. May he always be here among us; may he nurture our love for each other, share in our joys, and comfort us in our sorrows. Inspired by his teachings and example, let us seek to make our home before all else a dwelling place of love, diffusing far and wide the goodness of Christ."

Father Campbell smiled, nodding to June that it was her turn to read.

"A reading from the letter of St. Paul to the Colossians." Her voice trembled a little before gaining strength. "You are God's chosen race, his saints; He loves you, and you should be clothed in sincere compassion, in kindness and humility, gentleness and patience. Bear with one another; forgive each other as soon as a quarrel begins. The Lord has forgiven you; now you must do the same. Over all these clothes, to keep them together and complete them, put on love. And may the peace of Christ reign in your hearts, because it is for this that you were called together as parts of one body. Always be thankful.

"Let the message of Christ, in all its richness, find a home with you. Teach each other, and advise each other, in all wisdom. With gratitude in your hearts sing psalms and hymns and inspired songs to God; And never say or do anything except in the name of the Lord Jesus, giving thanks to God the Father through him. The word of the Lord."

"Thanks be to God," replied Lillian, Michael, and Father Campbell.

"O God, you fill the hungry with good things." The priest once more took the lead. As he spoke, he sprinkled holy water throughout the room. "Send your blessing on us, as we work in this kitchen, and make us ever thankful for our daily bread. Grant this through Christ Our Lord."

The family paused, looking around cautiously.

Nothing happened.

They snapped out of their momentary loss of focus. "Amen," they answered almost simultaneously.

"What room should we go to next?" he asked.

"Well, we're here on the first floor. Why not the dining room?" June suggested.

"Sounds good to me."

XXXVII

June led the group out of the kitchen and into the dining room. Father Campbell moved about the spacious room, flicking holy water throughout as he began to pray.

"Blessed are you, Lord of heaven and earth, for you give us food and drink to sustain our lives and make our hearts glad. Help us to be grateful for all your mercies, and mindful of the needs of others. Grant this through Christ Our Lord."

"Amen," came the response.

June sniffled as Father Campbell made the sign of the cross, finishing the blessing of the dining room. "He's gone," she said.

The priest turned and looked at her. "How-how do you know?"

"I don't know." June shrugged. "Sa—" she caught herself before she said her mentor's name. "Through research, I've learned that a place can be haunted by more than one lost soul. Especially one with history like this place. There was a suicide on the property, and a woman had an illegal abortion here and died. Throughout the blessing, I felt a male presence. By the time you finished, he was gone."

Lillian and Michael shuffled nervously as June spoke. Lillian's expression was that of a bored child waiting for a tedious chore to be over, and Michael could not hide his unease.

The priest hesitated before continuing, his face slightly drained of its natural color. The group moved toward Lillian's office. He blessed the hallways as he went. Arriving in the office, he began his prayer.

"O God, in your wise providence, you are glad to bless all human labor, the work of our hands and of our minds. Grant that all who plan and conduct business in this office may, through your guidance and support, come to the right decisions and carry them out fairly. We ask this through Christ Our Lord."

"Amen," Michael and June responded.

Both looked toward Lillian who was instead grabbing her lower abdomen. She was doubled over, her face contorted. She collapsed to the floor, writhing in pain. Her family rushed to her side, and the priest made the sign of the cross and said a silent prayer.

"What is happening, honey?" Michael asked, his voice anxious and filled with fear.

"I-I don't know!" she squealed in agony. "It-it hurts!" Tears streamed from her eyes.

June ran out of the room. She came back with a cool, wet washcloth for her mother's head.

Lillian's eyes had gone wide. "Why? No, you don't know!" she cried out and whimpered. "Yes, you don't understand."

June's eyes followed her mother's toward her unseen assailant. The faint image of a young woman formed. June couldn't be sure if she saw it with her eyes or perceived it with her mind.

"I have heard of this. She is under spiritual attack," the priest said, taking a vial of anointing oil from his pocket and beginning to recite a blessing for healing hands. "Yours are the hands full of experience and skill. Yours are the hands reaching out with compassion, taking time to show care, swiftly taking action."

"It's like a knife!" Lillian screamed while languishing on the floor.

"Yours are the hands gently touching your patients," Father Campbell continued, battling with the spirit. "You touch families, too. Yours are the hands that show you care. You lift the hearts of those who suffer. Your hands celebrate the joy of healing. Your hands bless all they touch with the spirit of compassion."

June held the cold compress to her mother's head. Michael held her hand, a bewildered and helpless expression on his face. Lillian had been reduced to a sobbing mess, curling into the fetal position in an attempt to stop the agony. Her knuckles and Michael's fingers were going white from the grip she had on his hand.

"Thank you for sharing your abundance and gifts, for touching lives and lifting spirits. Blessings and thanks for the many works of your hands. May your hands bring healing to all those you touch." In the palm of the hand not being held by her husband, the priest made the sign of the cross with his anointing oil.

"Why?" Michael asked, fear and anger mixing in his voice. "Why is this happening to her?"

"I don't know," Father Campbell said, his voice showing the strain from his prayers not working. He closed his eyes. "In the Name of Jesus Christ, Our God and Lord, strengthened by the intercession of the Immaculate Virgin Mary, Mother of God, of Blessed Michael the Archangel, of the Blessed Apostles Peter and Paul and all the Saints. And powerful in the holy authority of our ministry, we confidently undertake to repulse the attacks and deceits of the devil."

Lillian squirmed, breaking the hold Michael had on her hand to grasp at her abdomen. She started to sob. "I'm sorry! I'm so sorry!"

"Sorry about what?" Father Campbell asked.

Michael looked at her confused.

"I did what I had to do! I was doing what I was told! I shouldn't have had to," she moaned. "It's not my fault. I had to. I had to!" she cried out before breaking into blubbering sobs on the floor. She buried her face in her hands and curled back into the fetal position.

Stunned, the priest stood up as Michael lifted his wife off the floor.

"I'm going to take her to our room," Michael said as Lillian cried into his shoulder.

"I don't think we should stop the blessing half done. June and I can finish." He looked around uncertainly. "I think."

"Yeah, that would be great," Michael said softly, already halfway out of the room.

"I think," he said, turning his attention to June, "I may contact one of my friends who is a full-time exorcist and see if he can help. But first, let's take a look at the basement."

XXXVIII

"Is there a special prayer for basements?" June asked as she escorted the priest to their basement.

He chuckled. "No, more of a general prayer."

"Too bad. This basement could use all the help it can get." She opened the door and illuminated the area around them with her phone, taking a deep breath. "Ready, Father?"

He nodded. "Yes. But first, do you sense anything?"

She closed her eyes and meditated like Sara-Lyn taught her. "I have never liked it down here. I always feel like someone is watching me and wants me gone. I feel rage."

The priest headed down first, and June followed. He spritzed the stairs as he went. "Here, O God, may this household store its belongings, enjoy recreation, we pray with—" Suddenly he fell to his knees and tumbled down the stairs, crying out in pain, pressing his hand to his head.

"Father!" June ran to his side. "What's wro—" she stopped mid-sentence and looked up.

Standing there was a frontiersman. Fury emanated from his face as his gaze concentrated on the crumpled priest. There was a hole in the middle of his forehead. Her gaze moved from his horrid face to his hands, his right index finger decayed and showing exposed bone.

She suppressed a shudder. "What are you?" June asked, the presence of the priest and her family filling her with confidence.

In an instant, his evil gaze turned from Father Campbell to June. He extended a finger toward her, pointing to her forehead.

June stood her ground, afraid but empowered. "Is the legend Sara-Lyn told me true? Were you once a settler killed by raiders?" With each question, her confidence built and her fear diminished. "Or are you something evil?"

The phantom grinned, and then it felt like her brain was being cleaved in two. She gripped her head as the splitting headache incapacitated her. She dropped to her knees next to the priest, clutching her head. Her voice joined with the priests as they cried in agony.

"Mommy? I hear—" Mikey's voice pierced the darkness from the top of the stairs. "What's the bad man doing to you?"

"Mikey! Run!" June managed to scream as she saw the ghoul turn toward her son. But before he could run away, June heard the horrible, painful scream no mother should ever hear as Mikey fell.

XXXIX

Gently cradling his wife, Michael awkwardly used one hand to turn the doorknob to their bedroom. With a little shove, the door opened, and he carried Lillian to the bed and carefully lowered her to the mattress. He kissed her forehead.

"Is the priest still here?" Lillian asked.

"Yes, he and June are heading to the basement to cleanse it."

"I want him gone. I'm tired of this fucking supernatural bullshit. It's just a shared delusion. Nothing real," she said, clearly denying what she had just felt.

"Lillian, honey, he's here to help. That would be rude. He's a good fri—"

"I want him gone!" she yelled. "Fuck! A Catholic priest over your wife?"

"Okay, okay. He's gone. I'll go ask him to leave," he said, acquiescing to her demand as he stood.

"I'm going to shower," Lillian said.

"Okay."

The bathroom door shut behind Lillian as she turned on the water. As Michael reached the bedroom door, he heard his daughter cry out.

"Mikey! Run!"

Stunned, Michael himself broke into a run. He bounded down the stairs, turned a corner, and saw his grandson rolling on the ground, clutching his head and sobbing. Michael scooped his grandson into his arms and ran straight into the living room. As he got the child farther away from the top of the stairs, he seemed to stop crying.

"Mommy! Help Mommy, Paw-Paw!" he cried out.

"It's okay. It's okay." He kissed the boy's forehead. "I want you to stay right here, okay?"

Mikey nodded. Michael left him, running to his daughter without waiting for the child's reply.

§

June could barely make out the silhouette of her son at the top of the staircase. "Please! Kill me! Take me! Don't hurt my son!" she begged.

In response, the specter grinned until a shadow darkened the doorway.

June saw her father scooping up her son and hurrying him to safety. She rolled off her knees, collapsing back onto the floor. The next thing she knew, Michael was bounding down the stairs two at a time. He swept her up off the ground, and June noticed how he shivered when they passed through the ghastly figure.

The spirit, now even more enraged, turned to watch his prey escape. Then his expression changed. He was terrified.

June saw him open his mouth in a silent scream before she passed out of view. She only felt safe once Michael set her on the couch next to her son.

§

Michael found his friend clutching his head. The priest recoiled as Michael bent over to help him to his feet.

Father Campbell's eyes were wide with abject terror. "It—the pain. It hurt," the priest stammered. "Then, gone—stopped. Suddenly." He clutched his head, rubbing it with the palm of his hand. After a few deep breaths, Father Campbell looked up. "Michael? Can you help me up? I want to," he hesitated, "get the hell out of here." He paused once more. "No offense."

"Sure thing," Michael said, offering him his hand and helping him to his feet. "I'll make you some coffee and—"

"No, no, no," he said, cutting off his host. "Seriously, I just want to get the hell out of your house."

"Are you sure you are safe to drive?"

"No, but—"

Michael looked him in the eye. "You want to get the hell out of here?"

§

The hot water felt good on Lillian's body as she washed the stress away. There were going to be repercussions for her outburst. Luckily, it had only been her family and the priest, but she still sneered at the thought.

"Get a grip, Lillian. He was here to help," she said to herself as the scented body wash and massage of the shower calmed her rage. "Besides, they have a responsibility to keep their mouths shut, right?"

Still, a weight had been lifted from her shoulders. She felt lighter. Michael had carried her to bed and kissed her. She could tell he was more concerned for her than anything.

"Perhaps I could tell June why I kept Neil away," she mused.

It would be difficult to admit that, beyond her fears of Neil's behavior, she was just as terrified that June would eventually choose him over her. And that she just wanted Neil out of their lives and did not want to deal with his opinions on raising their daughter.

I don't have to admit to killing him.

The water began to turn cold.

"Nevermind," she chided herself. "You're being silly. He was an ass. Good riddance to bad rubbish. It's best to let sleeping dogs lie."

Lillian heard Father Campbell's car speeding away as she stepped out of the shower. She felt better. She wrapped a towel around her and put on her glasses. Once more, she froze in place. She watched as famil-

iar letters formed on the steamed vanity mirror: TELL
TRUTH.

XL

June came to a short time later with a still passed-out Mikey desperately clinging to her. Her mother was kneeling next to her and playing with her hair, a very unsettled look on her face.

Seeing June's eyes open, Lillian leaned over and kissed her forehead. "How are you doing, June-Bug?"

"I-I'm okay, Mom." She pulled her son to her, tightly embracing him. "How are you?" she asked, concerned.

"I have been better."

"Do you want to talk about it?"

"Don't be ridiculous. There's nothing to talk about," Lillian bit back before promptly getting up and leaving the room.

June opened her mouth to reply but closed it as Mikey stirred.

It's not worth the battle. Not today.

Not since June had a feeling that she knew exactly what the spirits tried to make her mother admit.

As June's gaze trailed across the room, she caught a glimpse of Mikey's bear with its sad eyes sitting just inside the doorway. She closed her eyes, not wanting to deal with anything else at the moment. She was done with ghosts and spirits and poltergeists. She just wanted to sleep.

Michael offered to carry Mikey upstairs to bed, but June was feeling clingy for her child.

"Good night. I love you guys," June said, as if all were as usual.

"Good night, June," Michael said lovingly.

"Sweet dreams, honey," Lillian replied.

June entered the bedroom and closed the door with her foot. She crossed the room and set the softly snoring Mikey down. She realized they'd left the bear downstairs—he never went to bed without it. She thought about going and getting it, but, to be honest, it creeped her out a little. And the boy was sleeping *deeply*, so she just curled up around him.

For all of her exhaustion, she couldn't quiet her mind. She knew from her studies with Sara-Lyn that the ghosts had been tied to the house in life. Now that she was armed with knowledge, she understood that the emotional upheaval of the dissolution of her marriage and her return to this house was powerful enough fuel for whatever was manifesting itself.

As June's mind gave way to sleep, she dreamed of the house she shared with Robert in Atlanta. But it soon turned into the hotel room where she had first seen him with the other woman. She was devastated. Then she was angry.

Knock. Knock. Knock.

Her eyes sprang open. But as she sat up, the sounds stopped. She leaned down and kissed her son. Whatever it was she was generating through her emotions, she would not let it affect Mikey after the day he'd had. Quietly, she slid out of the bed and crept out of the room. Closing the door behind her, she was going to go back to her room and try to sleep again, but she wanted to make a call.

"Hello, June. How'd the exorcism go?" Sara-Lyn's voice was alert if not a little tinny over the phone.

"Horrible and incredible all at the same time. I stood up to the ghosts!"

"Do you think you got them all?"

"No." June sighed. "I felt two, a man and a woman leave. But in the basement—it was too powerful. Honestly, I don't know if there's something more than a ghost down there. It felt different. Do you think an inhuman entity could be feeding off me? Wouldn't a medium make a juicy snack? Keep it strong?"

"Yes. However, I don't think it's feeding off you. You're drawn to the light," Sara-Lyn explained. "You have The Circle, and Wahchinksapa revealed himself to you."

"But then who?" June's voice trailed.

"I think you know the answer already."

June shook her head at the truth she already knew. "This doesn't mean—" June stopped herself from saying "we." "This doesn't mean that Emily was right about her being a murderer."

"No, it doesn't, but it does mean you need to be careful." Sara-Lyn's voice cracked. "I wish I could be there. You need someone to have your back, but I would just make things more tense and complicated. If Lillian is under the influence of something inhuman, she could be more dangerous than you're prepared for."

"I'll be careful."

"I hope so. I'll be praying for you—in my own way," Sara-Lyn said, her voice thick with worry. "Call me in the morning."

"I will," June promised. "I need to go. Good night."

"Good night, June."

XLI

As June stepped out of the bathroom, far too awake for her liking, the sound of rustling in the kitchen drew her attention. She started to stealthily move downstairs almost on instinct. Her heart pounded, afraid of what she would encounter but a bit braver after the day's events.

When she saw the shadow of her mother, June breathed a sigh of relief. "Mom?" she softly called out.

The shadow stopped. "Yes, dear?" Lillian called from the kitchen.

"Everything all right?" she asked, picking up momentum as she headed toward the kitchen, curious as to why her mother was awake until she heard a shrill whistle.

"Yes, dear. Want a cup?" Lillian asked, looking to her daughter.

"Please," June said, going to grab a mug for herself.

"Here, I got it. Go sit."

June relaxed as she took a seat at the table. Despite her fears of the entity that could be feeding off her mother, she knew Lillian's strongest instinct had always been to take care of her family. Even when she was an obnoxious teenager, her mother was there for her. Throughout all the trials and tribulations of her various illnesses growing up, Lillian was always there, protecting her and watching over her. When she was in middle school, she had nominated Lillian to be Mother of the Year for the state of Missouri. Lillian had won.

"Mom, thank you," June said as her mother prepared the tea.

"For what?" Lillian asked, reaching for her daughter's favorite mug. She pulled a vial of June's medicine out of the cabinet, emptied the contents into the tea, and stirred.

"For being there for me growing up. Even when I became an obnoxious teenager. I never really grew out of it until I got pregnant and married." She paused, trying to fight the tears. "But you handled me with so much ... grace. I don't know how you did it without throttling me." She sniffled and wiped away a tear. "I only hope that when Mikey gets to be that age, I'm half the mother you are."

Lillian was beaming as she sat down across from her daughter. She reached out and patted June's hand.

"You will be." She then slid June her mug. "Now drink up so you can get some sleep."

"Okay, Mom," she said, her voice suddenly childlike.

Her concerns about the entity slipped away. For the moment, things had calmed. Maybe she would bring up the entity they had not exorcized later when they weren't so beat. June brought the mug to her lips when her hands began to shake, the cup frozen an inch from her face.

Lillian finished taking her sip and looked at her daughter quizzically. "What's wrong, dear?"

"I-I-I don't know. I can't move my arms. What's happening?" June's eyes were wide with fear as she fought to move. She felt like something was holding her in place. "Why can't I move my arms, Momma?" she cried out.

Lillian started to rise when her mug slipped from her hands and crashed to the floor, shattering and spilling its contents on the kitchen tile. She was forced back into her chair by a force as powerful as it was invisible. Now Lillian's eyes were open wide.

One by one June's fingers were pried from the mug. The vessel hung in midair and June's hands were pushed aside. Slowly, the cup floated over the table from daughter to mother. As it drew near, Lillian tightly shut her mouth, sealing her lips and shaking her head.

"Tell. Truth! Admit." The voice was unfamiliar and loud. "Lillian!" The disembodied voice insisted, filled with righteous wrath.

The cup moved closer to her lips, but Lillian remained defiant. Her eyes were tightly shut.

"Lillian!" This time the sound of her name caused Lillian to open her eyes wide.

June watched as her mother's eyes welled with tears. The cup lowered itself to the table. Lillian struggled to move, to bat the cup away, but she couldn't. All she could do was speak.

"June, there is something I need to tell you about your father."

XLI

"I killed him." Lillian's voice quivered, and her eyes glistened with tears before turning hard. "You don't know him like I do. I had to protect you."

"The fuck you did!" June slammed a fist on the table, her mother gasping at the outburst.

Lillian took a moment to collect herself before shouting back. "The fuck I didn't! Everything I have ever done is for you! That is the role of a mother! And the ingratitude of our children is our torment!"

"Why? What made you do this?"

Lillian scoffed at the tears running down June's face. "You contacted him!" Lillian's voice burned with rage. "You ignored my wishes when all I wanted was to protect you! To protect our family!" Lillian's tone turned cold. She shrugged. "It was self-defense."

"Maybe he was messed up once, but he got his life together!" June's voice had regained some of its strength. "He remarried! He had two more kids! When

I reached out to him, he was kind and gentle. You robbed me of knowing him!" June growled. "I love you, but you have to pay for what you did. This is not just about me anymore. You must face justice."

Lillian's stare bored into her daughter, and she laughed. "Oh, and you would turn your own mother in?" She glanced up and saw a figure darkening the door to the kitchen.

It was Michael, his mouth agape. He immediately turned and ran.

The women, still frozen in place, heard the door to the master suite slam shut.

Lillian, unbothered, returned her gaze to June. "You would've brought a mean, cruel man back into all of our lives! And to include your son! He would have just disappointed you. Remember what I told you? About how he shook me? Abused me? Think of Mikey and what he could've done to him! This was self-defense. If you think about it," Lillian almost smirked again, "it's all your fault."

June's mouth dropped open.

"Lies!" The voice boomed again.

It was then that a middle-aged man appeared, standing in the middle of the table. Too angry to deal with the unreality of the apparition, Lillian screamed in frustration. June's awestruck face enraged her further.

"You were so angry, Lillian. I thought you were going to wake June! I was trying to hold you!" His face fell. "But that doesn't matter now."

"Dad?" June asked. "Is-is it true? She did this?"

Lillian couldn't believe June's betrayal, choosing Neil over her yet again.

Neil turned to June. "Yes, June-Bug." He reached out and caressed her face.

June closed her eyes as he did so.

"But that's not important now," Neil started. "What is important is you stay strong for what comes next." He turned back to Lillian. "Tell her the truth. Admit that so much of what you told her about me was a lie. Tell her how you forced me to sign away my parental rights under threat of arrest! Tell her how hard I tried to see her! For once in your life, just be honest!"

Lillian was all silent rage.

"I didn't think so," Neil said as he reached out for June's tea. He lifted it once more to Lillian's lips. "This isn't even the stuff that you have been giving her, is it? This is pure poison! You were going to kill her!" Neil shouted, furious.

Lillian's face became impassive. "I am a good mother, and you're an abusive prick," she said calmly.

His eyes flickered with rage. "For once in your life, tell the fucking truth! Admit what you've done and take responsibility!" His voice roared and shook the walls.

"Daddy, stop it! I'm scared!"

Neil's face fell. "June-Bug," he said softly, turning back to look at her.

"No!" Lillian's shrill, screeching voice pierced the room.

Neil writhed in agony, the cup of tea clattering to the table, forgotten.

Lillian had stood up, the darkness backing her and overpowering Neil's hold on her. "You will not take my daughter away from me!"

"Mother," June said coldly, standing up. "Is there poison in that cup?"

"Absolutely not! Don't you remember? I was Mother of the Year!" Lillian said, suddenly sounding injured and meek. "You were sick so often; people didn't know how we kept everything together—how *I* kept everything together. I won Mother of the Year!" Lillian's voice hardened once more. "And now you attack me? Because a ghost told you so? You're going to choose him over me?" Angry tears streamed down Lillian's face.

"Mom, I just want to hear you say it."

The lights flickered on and off.

"You don't believe me? You would betray your own *mother*?" she growled.

"Answer the question, Lillian," Neil commanded. "Why is it so hard to admit?"

She looked at her ex-husband. The light seemed to bend around her, shrouding her in shadow. "This is your fault. This is *all your fault*!" she shrieked. "You ruined my life! You failed in life and now you haunt me—us—in death? Huh? Is that it?"

The butcher's block at her left began to move, tremble, and empty itself of its knives.

"It's not going to work, Lillian," he said. "You know what I am. You know what exists; you just never acknowledged it. Your skeptical nature wouldn't allow it."

"Mom, are you doing that with the knives?" June asked.

Neil spoke when Lillian did not. "The darkness in the basement. You've felt it, June. It—he is funneling through your mother. The evil has controlled her for a long time now, probably since she was a child." He looked back at Lillian.

The knives began spinning.

"Please. You can't hurt me any longer," Neil continued.

"Momma, please. You're scaring me," June said as she tried to stand, only to be forced back into her chair. "Daddy, did you do that?"

He looked over his shoulder. "No, June-Bug."

The knives spun faster.

"Please, Lillian, stop this."

A flash of awareness flickered across Lillian's face, and the knives slowed. June squirmed.

"Neil," Lillian started. "You hurt me. Your anger." A tear slid down her cheek.

"I'm sorry, Lillian. I had to wrestle with my own demons. I wasn't the perfect husband."

Lillian's features briefly softened.

"But I got better," Neil pressed. "You can, too."

The anger returned to Lillian's face. "Get better? Get better! I'm not the abusive asshole! Everything *I've* done has been justified."

The knives picked up speed.

"Every. Time." She smiled wickedly.

"Lillian! Stop!" he cried out as she grabbed a knife from midair and lunged at him, stabbing wildly. He howled in horror as the knife passed through him and sank into the soft flesh of June's abdomen.

June didn't even look to her wound. She looked into Lillian's eyes. "Momma, why?" She slid to the floor, clutching at the knife.

Lillian's eyes widened. This was not the plan. This was going to fall on *her*. She swore she felt a hand on her shoulder.

"Lillian, save her!" It was Neil. "You can do this!"

"No!" she wailed in frenzied resentment. She stood up. "*You* did this, you son of a bitch! Why did you have to come back? Why did you have to harass me? *You* fucking attacked *me*!" She kicked at him. "*You* pushed me over the edge when we were married! *You* are the one who drove me nuts! Made me crazy!"

"Momma," June's voice was hoarse as tears began streaming down her face. "You admit it."

Lillian turned to her daughter, not fully realizing what June was referring to. "I admit your father was a monster! He's the one who pushed me. Why was I the mother *and* provider? He was the man, but he couldn't keep a job! He pushed me to go to medical school because somebody had to make good money!"

"But you said," June paused, fingering the blood soaking her shirt, "you'd wanted to be a doctor since you were a little girl?"

"Yes." Lillian slowly, maternally, advanced on her. "I did. But then I had you." She knelt, slowly reaching for the knife. "I wanted to be a mother once *he* put you in my arms. Then I wanted you and motherhood to be my world! But then he lost his job. Then he lost his second job. I knew then I had to give up being a mother. *I* had to be the professional one." Her hands gripped the knife handle. "It was so much stress. I did not know what I was doing. I-I would black out. But it's all right now! Momma is here. She'll take care of everything."

June gasped in pain as Lillian began to remove the knife from her stomach. "Momma, please. Don't. I don't wanna go," June sobbed.

"Lillian! No!"

§

Michael's mind reeled as he wrapped his head around what was happening to his family. He wept as he bounded up the stairs, trying to figure out what to do next. He saw his grandson's door open.

"Paw-Paw, what's wrong?" he asked sleepily.

"It's okay, buddy," Michael said, grabbing him and carrying him back to bed. "I need you to stay here, okay?"

"Mommy. I want my mommy." He started to cry.

Michael grabbed the child and held him close to his chest. "It's okay. Listen, I'm going to go get your mommy." He rocked the child to calm him down. As he did, he could hear the conversation echoing through the ductwork of the home's HVAC system. What he heard chilled him. "Listen, let's play a game. I want you to hide under your bed and not come out until your mother or I come for you, okay?"

"Grandma, too?" he said, brightening.

"No, buddy. Grandma is it. She'll tag you, and then you'll be it and you'll lose the game." He studied the child's expression. "If you hear Grandma, I want you to be very still and quiet. Think you can do that?"

Mikey nodded yes.

"Ready? Go!"

Giggling, the toddler scurried under his bed.

Michael sprinted out of the child's room, shutting the door behind him. He dug through his sock drawer looking for his handgun case. Finding it, he unlocked it and took out the .357 revolver before scavenging for ammunition. As he scavenged, he grabbed his cell from his nightstand and, putting it on speaker, called 911. With trembling hands, he loaded the cylinder. His heart was racing, and he felt like he was all thumbs. Several of the jacketed hollow point rounds did not make it in on the first try. He could hear the cries of pain and anger from downstairs. He was already hating himself for what he knew he had to do.

§

Neil knew that, if he did not act, Lillian would finish pulling the knife from his daughter's abdomen, causing her to bleed out. The evil was thick around her, and he felt fear. He did not know if it would absorb him or drain him. Either way, he knew that it would end him.

But if he did not act—if he did not risk the dangers of the darkness—his daughter would die. And he couldn't lose her again.

He lunged at his ex-wife, using every bit of his strength to pry her fingers from the knife. As they slipped off the handle, he pulled her across the room and away from June. He felt the darkness wrestling with him, Lillian's anger and fear. Her wild flailing made it difficult for him to hold onto her. He summoned his voice.

"June! Get out of here!"

§

June struggled to her feet. Her first thought was to go to her son's room, but, even in her disoriented state, she realized the sight of her would traumatize Mikey and lead Lillian straight to him. She hurried out the door, trying to stand as straight as possible and move as quickly as possible when all she wanted to do was double over and hope help arrived before it was too late.

She had to get to The Circle. She brushed past her mother. Lillian reached for her as she staggered by, clutching at thin air. June heard Michael coming downstairs as she opened the door. She hoped he would know where to find her.

She collapsed as soon as she reached The Circle. She heard a gunshot. She thought she heard sirens. As she felt her eyes closing, she thought she could feel the comfort and warmth of a blanket covering her.

Epilogue

JUNCTION FALLS, MO — Local physician Lillian Reuter, M.D., was judged not guilty by reason of insanity today in the abuse of a minor, poisoning, and attempted murder of her daughter, June Williams. Following a house blessing by a Catholic priest, Dr. Reuter suffered a nervous breakdown and admitted to having been poisoning Ms. Williams since she was a child. Dr. Reuter then attacked her daughter with a kitchen knife, stabbing her in the abdomen. The attack was stopped only when Dr. Reuter's husband, Michael Reuter, shot the physician.

Dr. Reuter's attorneys have suggested that she did not understand the morality of her actions due to the disease Induced Illness by Caregivers. This disorder used to be known as Munchausen by Proxy.

290

These cases are rare, and those who exhibit symptoms often don't seek material gain for their actions. Instead, they seek positive attention. At this time, Dr. Reuter has yet to be diagnosed with any emotional or mental disorder. She is currently placed at the Wyldewood Behavioral Health Facility.

On the question of the alleged murder of her ex-husband, Neil Vincent of Beaumont, Kentucky, authorities are currently awaiting results from tissue samples following the exhumation of his remains. Originally, Mr. Vincent's family opposed the exhumation until credit card records revealed Dr. Reuter had purchased fuel two miles from the residence where he was found dead of an apparent heart attack.

Wyldewood Behavioral Health Facility

Lillian rocked herself in her room as she waited for the drugs to kick in. Though she had survived being shot by Michael, she had not emerged unscathed. The bullet nicked her spine, paralyzing her from the waist down. Now she spent most of her time institutionalized, staring into the distance. For the most part, she was silent. But every once in a while, she talked to herself. Sometimes she spoke to people no one else saw.

Occasionally, she would be apologetic for her crimes and express genuine sorrow. Occasionally. For the most part, she blamed others for her current predicament. It was her former husband who had pushed her over the edge, both when he was alive and when his ghost defied death to vex her. It was her daughter that had betrayed her and chosen a deadbeat and absent father over the woman who had sacrificed so much for her. And then the worst betrayal: Her husband shot her, sentencing her to spend the rest of her life in this chair.

The other patients avoided her, as did most of the staff. Dr. Wackerfuss refused to participate in her care the moment he learned of what she had done, citing that the harm she caused to one of his previous patients would interfere with his ability to provide her with the best care. Wyldewood's administrators and attorneys agreed and assigned her to another caregiver. She had never liked Wackerfuss.

She hated the orderlies; she had to boss them around like she was still the physician and not the patient. She doubted the credentials of the social workers, psychologists, and psychiatrists who attempted to treat her. Therefore, she was left alone often, like this afternoon.

No one noticed the butter knife she had snuck out of the dining facility. No one noticed as she slowly sharpened it day after day. So, no one noticed when she cut herself. June would've been proud.

§

Since her release from the hospital, Lillian spent most of her time in her office. It was different now. June and Mikey had moved out and were living in a trailer on Sara-Lyn's property. That Michael allowed this only made Lillian angrier. More so because the witch even visited the house with June and Mikey. It enraged her almost as much as seeing how her misery seemed to make June and Mikey *happy*.

Michael had changed. He was remarkably calm in her presence. Her belongings had been boxed up; Michael had decided to sell the home, ignoring her objections. Most of her stuff had been sold to pay the hospital and legal bills. Her family had been ignoring her since she came home, pretending she wasn't even there. It hurt, and some days it made her angry.

Most days it made her angry.

Especially when they excluded her from family events, like visiting the cemetery where her parents were buried. She would obviously like to pay a visit to her parents' graves, but they didn't seem to think about what she wanted. Instead, she had to watch from her office window, helpless in her wheelchair, as Michael, June, Mikey, and that annoying Emily stood before a headstone, all of them dressed in black.

Acknowledgments

For as much as writing is a solitary endeavor, to be fully successful it has to be social as well. Writers never finish a manuscript solely upon their own effort: There's workshopping, beta reading, editing, and (most importantly) lifting each other up when the words just won't come. The following were instrumental in the completion of this novel:

The story revealed itself to me in 2018 while I was sicker than I have ever been in my life. I couldn't sleep and had gone a little wonky in my misery. So, I guess whatever horrid microbe tortured my body and mind for a week deserves first credit.

That leads me to Morticia, my #1 Emotional Support Human, the wonderful woman who helped nurse me back to health and has dealt with the ups and downs that come with my being an author.

Next is my first reader and muse, Derek (aka Dare-Bear). Your cheerleading and support helped me create the best version of this story. Not only did you lift me up when I was feeling like an imposter or stuck—you spoke truth even when I sucked! If I don't suck as a writer, it's because of you.

David, thank you for beta reading and helping with Tarot research! *Beginner's Guide to Tarot* by Juliet Sharman-Burke and illustrated by Giovanni Caselli and *Kitchen Table Tarot: Pull Up a Chair, Shuffle the Cards, and Let's Talk Tarot* by Melissa Cynova were great suggestions!

In trying to figure out my next move, I found Emerson College and their online MFA in Popular Fiction Writing and Publishing. This program gave me the tools and networking to successfully go indie with my writing. I want to give a shout-out to my peers: Sara, Deanna, Rachelle, Alanna, Doug, and Michael. Thank you for all the honest feedback and friendship. Then there's an amazing cadre of professors: Kevin, Edwin, Jon, and Gian. Thank you for all the encouragement. This novel would not be the same without your guidance throughout my time there.

After graduating, I submitted the manuscript to Raquel Pidal's editing capstone class. Two students picked me for their capstone project. The first was Lillian. I hope that you enjoy the final product! That's also where I met Kayla, who became my permanent editor. Since then, we have gone on quite the journey together! We have created something both of us should be proud of. Here's to many more stories to tell.

I also want to thank Corey for joining me on this journey. It is always amazing to see you bring my stories to life! While not included in this book (even if it ties into it!), the image of June under the streetlamp that inspired the cover hits me directly in the feels.

Then there's Paul J. & Nikki McSorely, who gave me my first break on "Fear From The Heartland." And Paul is doing the audiobook of this novel! It gives me chills to hear my stories told in Paul's voice.

Alea, your design gives my books the professional look and feel that proves indie authors and presses can hang with the big publishing houses! Congratulations on your recent graduation—I know you'll go far!

Rick, this is an amazing cover! Thank you for your patience as I've figured out the publishing end of writing. Did I mention how absolutely blown away I am by this cover?

Sally, your trailers are absolutely fabulous! Each time I've placed an order, I've waited with bated breath to see how you are going to turn my text into a video! And each time, I'm impressed with how much they rival those of big-name authors!

I cannot forget my parents who gave me life, without whom none of this would be possible. And to my grandparents, without whom my parents wouldn't have been possible. Especially my mom's parents for her blindness, without which I would not exist.

Lynne and Rich, there is just so much. As I wrote this, Lynne was one of the readers I had in mind, and I did my best to get the technical stuff right with the paranormal. And thank you for introducing me to *The Soul of the Indian* by Charles Alexander Eastman, which made an appearance. Rich, that you read this and liked it means so much to me. That I could capture your attention makes me feel like I have a shot at this career.

Genie, thank you for being my #1 fan and cheerleader! Sorry if I haven't always been the most communicative, but you were there for me on one of the worst days of my life.

Jim, thank you for buying multiple copies of my books for your neighborhood's Little Free Libraries.

Tena and John, thank you for the lasagna during my and Morticia's (first) battle with COVID! And then helping Dad and me with the celebration.

Don and Jenny, thank you for being there that cold February night.

Jan and Butch, thank you for reminding me that Mom lives not only within me but within the many children she taught.

Sandy and Mike, thank you for all the times you reached out and kept us in your thoughts and prayers.

Then there's the family you pick. Chris, Kim, Glen, and Hannah, thank you for all your love and support as I've undertaken this crazy adventure! To my fellow P40 alums, it was a pleasure working side by side with you in the meme mines. If there's ever an XPK fan club, I'm pretty sure the first president will be from this group!

Mike, thank you for all the guidance and insight into this new world of writing and publishing. You introduced me to the concept of Tuckerizing, which I have had *way* too much fun with!

Shannon, at MM 218 a guy named I met someone named U who was trying to get her car fixed at Rolf's "Meh" Service but the station is now closed. Go figure! (Note: My editor is not responsible for the grammatical anomaly that is the preceding acknowledgment!)

Ms. Reed and Mrs. Springer, you helped keep my dream of being an author alive, through both encouraging me to write and exposing me to literature.

XPK

COMING SOON

Pea Ridge
A Novel by Xavier Poe Kane

Please enjoy a first look into Kane's next project.

Two days ago, on a dying planet far, far away …

A pair of six-legged, rodent-like creatures scurried through the dense underbrush of grassland. The female lagged the male, one leg having been broken when their burrow collapsed following one of the planetquakes that had become all too common. Now she and her mate had to find a new home, and her hearts pounded as she sensed multiple predators stalking her.

§

The creature watched as her son stalked the two rodents frantically zig-zagging through the tall grass. He crouched, ready to pounce whenever his mother gave him the signal.

She knew her son was focused on the female, as she was slower than the other from an injury that would heal in time. But his hunting instincts were still developing, so she telepathically probed his emotions and thoughts. She gave him a gentle nudge, sharing an image of the tiny embryos growing within the female rodent. This was followed by an image of the sickness growing in the male. Her son now understood that the male would be dead soon and the female would give birth after her leg healed.

Their kind had evolved to hunt only the sick and weak among their prey, leaving the healthy to procreate and increase their food supply. It was her duty to pass these lessons to her son, just as her mother had taught them to her. She felt her son's focus change to the male right before he pounced.

The kill was quick, the rodent barely able to squeal before being sucked into the tooth-lined maw of her son. The female squeaked in terror and took off running as best she could. The creature sensed her son's hunger, now more urgent with sustenance moving toward his belly. She willed her offspring to remain strong and resist his primal instinct to continue feeding. They were not like the other animals—they viewed themselves as shepherds of nature.

Her son's muscles tensed as his body arched, his limbs quivering as his brain calculated how far to jump to intercept the fleeing rodent. The creature calmed herself and projected that calm onto her son. As her muscles relaxed, so did his. Ignoring her own desire to feast, she reminded him of the evening's ritual and their duty to attend it.

The swarm worshiped the purple moon. They would rhythmically circle the sacred stones while waving sticks and sending positive waves toward the night's bringer of light. The elders could no longer hide their worry that the moon was upset with them, fearing she was the cause of the planetquakes that were destroying their environment. As the ritual finished, the moon momentarily went dark.

The mother-son pair looked skyward and saw a triangular craft silently come to a stop and lower until it was just off the ground. An extraordinary blue beam of light was projected under the object. A strange, bipedal figure gently descended.

The creature's son hid beneath her tail as the figure began walking their way. She hissed softly in warning, and the alien held up a hand. Studying the newcomer, she noted its gray skin, softened by the purple light, and the two shiny black eyes that studied her in return. It gently reached toward her and placed a hand on her head between her eye stalks. She was flooded with a profound sense of calm and peace before her world went dark.

TOP SECRET / DOE / POTUS EYES ONLY

EBEN Amb informed DOE of imminent
LEVEL ONE contact incident with disabled spacecraft relocating endan-
gered semi-sentient species. Species
assessed EXTREME HAZARD to PEOPLE
PROPERTY ENVIRONMENT. Projected impact site MISSOURI counties CRAWFORD
FRANKLIN GASCONADE. WMD-CST assis-
tance requested for en route DOE RRT.

NATO/RUS/CHI advised per ROSWELL AC-
CORDS.

Listen to Xavier Poe Kane on:

FEAR FROM THE HEARTLAND

Hosted by Paul J. McSorley

Season 3

Episode 2: Cosmic Creatures (Pea Ridge Part 1)
Episode 8: Wretched Reconstruction (Appalachia)
Episode 11: Cosmic Creatures (Pea Ridge Part 2)
Episode 15: Cosmic Creatures (Pea Ridge Part 3)
Halloween Special: The Last Bride
Episode 25: Naughty By Nature (Snaggle & Thor Save Christmas)

Season 4

Episode 2: Warfare and Werewolves (The Werewolf Truce)
Episode 6: Unwrapped Realities (Cadotte's Pass)
Episode 13: Flesh Fiasco (Suzanne)

Presented by:

CHILLING TALES
FOR DARK NIGHTS

Listen on YouTube or wherever you enjoy your Podcasts!

Printed in the USA
CPSIA information can be obtained
at www.ICGtesting.com
JSHW050340290324
60088JS00006B/11

9 798985 790511